THESE NOTES ARE AS DIFFERENT AS DAY AND NIGHT

UNITED STATES NOTE

FEDERAL RESERVE NOTE

HONE$T MONEY

CHARLES S. NORBURN, M.D.

NEW PURITAN LIBRARY
FLETCHER, NORTH CAROLINA

Library of Congress Catalog Card Number: 83-060478
ISBN 0-932050-19-0

NOTE

The bankers referred to in this book are not the friendly, helpful people who work in our local banks. The "bankers" we know perform honest service for modest, often meager salaries — far removed from the overlords.

No, I speak of great financiers, who see things in a global way, who have succeeded in obtaining claims for all the wealth of the nation and thirst for all the wealth in the world.

They have made laws giving them a right to strive for this wealth, get it, and hold it.

Special Acknowledgement

I wish to express my indebtedness and appreciation to:

Dr. Jack R. Ferber for his encouragement and advice.

Dr. Logan Robertson for the many periodicals he brought, and for his selfless and devoted care.

A long habit of not thinking a thing wrong gives it a superficial appearance of being right.

— *Thomas Paine*

Author's Preface

What a marvelous country was this new world.

AMERICA

Its coastline, dotted with deep harbors, seemed endless. It had great mountains and great rivers. There were magnificent forests and vast fertile plains. Its earth was rich with minerals.

Those who came to live in this veritable paradise were of sturdy stock. They were industrious, saving and ingenious. They had the best government ever devised.

How does it happen that now, after more than three hundred years of intense toil, the inhabitants of this nation find themselves more than ten trillion dollars in debt? They have received no benefits to justify this debt. To whom do they owe it? How were the claims acquired?

Earlier in life, I, like most people, was not concerned with the national economy. I vaguely felt that this was in good hands. I put my thoughts and efforts into my work as a surgeon.

Then there was a change. Some thirty years ago I was

disabled in an accident. Reduced to viewing newscasts and reading the news, I became increasingly aware of the growing debt, of the continuous concentration of wealth, of the worsening plight of most of our people and of the rapid decline of our nation from its once supreme position of world influence and power.

I saw also that other countries, following the same pattern were drifting into communism, socialism or fascism — all wealth held by a small ruling clique — most of the people without private property or personal freedom.

Searching for an explanation, I began to make notes and save news clippings. At first there were few related articles. Then, as inflation worsened, as interest rates, unemployment, welfare rolls, debts and taxes increased, there came more and more — thousands of them, not only of news but of complaint. Books on the subject began to appear.

Not one gave, for me, a satisfactory explanation of the cause of our trouble. Not one stated what I saw to be the truth — that any upswing in our economy would be followed by a still deeper decline. Not one offered a real solution.

Long study, tracing the causes of our troubles back and back, showed that almost all stemmed from a common origin — the bribery of public officials, who then placed our monetary system in the hands of a few financiers.

From my studies, and from my mass of clippings, I aim to give the reader a clear and full picture of our economic system; to alert him to the danger facing this nation; to show that our economic system will never right itself; that in general, the plight of our people will always worsen; and further, to show that halfway measures won't do; to give the basis for the reforms I propose — to justify them — to show their necessity.

I divide the study into two small books. This, the first,

deals with the private control of the nation's money, and a proposed reform.

The first reform step must be the repeal of the Federal Reserve Act of 1913. This must be decisive. If we allow the same type of men to devise the new system, or to run it, nothing will be gained. We must formulate a clear idea of what the new system should be.

The heart of the recommended monetary system is Lincoln's United States Note, used as the Massachusetts Colony used its note. Details of the system are given.

Relieved of high taxes, high and accumulating interest, and overwhelming debt, our people could use their earnings to build their lives.

My second book, *Honest Government,* will complete the report of my studies. It will tell how we can regain control of our government, and use its protection and its bounty for every citizen alike.

Envisioned here and shown step by step, is an almost tax-free society of free men; a government that would enrich the rank and file of its citizens, instead of pauperizing them — a society in which able bodied citizens could, without government harrassment and without government handouts, support themselves and their families and provide for their old age as once they did.

"Nor are we acting for ourselves alone, but for the whole human race" (Thomas Jefferson).

Foreword

Honest Money is a book whose time has come. It calls for the abolishing of the Federal Reserve System through repeal of the Federal Reserve Act of 1913. Since a bill has already been introduced in the House of Representatives to do that, this book should help to provide the massive education program necessary to get it passed.

Jim Townsend, chairman of the R.O.C. movement to "Redeem Our Country" by abolishing the Fed, says this will be the number one issue in the 1984 elections. No congressman will deserve the support of voters suffering under the crushing burden of debt-usury money, unless he advocates genuine monetary reform.

The day of control of the American economy by international banksters is nearly over. Ahead lies a glorious destiny for those who are able to rise to the challenge in these days of convulsive change.

Unfortunately, most of the hundreds of patriotic organizations calling for Constitutional money believe all of it must be gold- or silver-backed. With Rothschild-Rockefeller control of vast reserves of the world's gold, this would inevitably put the people under the same oppressive heels that maneuver the "Fed." In other words, it would guarantee America's jumping from the frying pan into the fire!

There is a better way. Dr. Charles Norburn, who has studied this issue for 30 years, has found that way in a return to the United States Note which saved the Union in our national crisis over a century ago. He joins very good company in this crusade — no less a statesman than Abraham Lincoln!

He has convinced me — a hard-boiled, gold-standard advocate for years — after many hours of editorial work on his manuscript. Read the incredible product of this brilliant mind and see if he does not convince *you!*

It has been well said that one cannot stop a stampeding herd, but he can turn it. *Honest Money* should be used of God to do just that. Everyone who is informed and determined to see America return to the Constitution wants the Fed abolished. *What happens afterward* will make all the difference.

Pat Brooks, author of
The Return of the Puritans

Contents

.

ILLUSTRATIONS

PRIVATE ISSUE
AND CONTROL
OF THE NATION'S
MONEY

*"No man, or set of men
are entitled to exclusive
or separate emoluments
or privileges
from the Community"*
(The Virginia Declaration of Rights,
May 27, 1776).

CHAPTER 1

The Origin of Paper Money

In primitive times a man in need of a particular article was obliged to search until he found an owner willing to trade for his goods or services.

Later, as desires widened, barter became even more difficult, and goods and services were often exchanged for some third commodity, not needed, but which could be more readily exchanged for the needed article. Many things were used as a go-between.

The Bible mentions money in Genesis 23:16, about 1830 B.C.

"Abraham weighed to Ephron the silver, which he had named in the audience of the sons of Heth, four hundred shekels of silver, current money with the merchant." Chapter 24:22 mentions gold shekels.

Gold became a favorite. It was used in adornment. It was imperishable. It was rare. It could easily be carried about and could be hidden in a jar in the ground. Gold had, therefore, a wider acceptance than, say, a pile of logs a man might be offered for his cattle.

Each man had to be his own judge as to purity and value

3

of the gold offered. It was, however, not gold that most people wanted. They wanted a dependable medium of exchange; a standard of value; a dependable storehouse of wealth; a standard for deferred payments. Only a government could create standardized money of compulsory acceptance, and after thousands of years one did.

One of the first coins was used by the Liddians, about 650 B.C. It was natural that their government would simply standardize the favorite go-between. The first coins were bean shaped, marked with a punch, and contained 75 percent gold and 25 percent silver.

Other countries soon brought out gold coins bearing images of their rulers. Thus, gold became the official money.

During the Middle Ages most people who had gold deposited it with goldsmiths (paying for its safekeeping) until it was needed to make a purchase. The goldsmiths would give these depositors claim checks or receipts for the gold. Of course, the goldsmiths could not lend these receipts. The owners of the gold took them to hold, to lend, or to use in making a purchase.

As anyone who held a receipt could go to the goldsmiths and get the gold, these receipts began to be used in trade. Soon, for convenience and for safety, the receipts (paper money) were used almost entirely and gold was rarely called for. This was a true one-hundred-percent Gold Reserve System. For every receipt there was gold in the vault to redeem it. The fault with the system was that its base (gold) was a commodity, and, as such, was owned and often hoarded by the wealthy; its use denied to many.

As people multiplied and as business increased, there came a time when the scarcity of gold and gold receipts caused severe hardship. Money as a medium of exchange had become a necessity of life. A way was found to increase it. In the 16th century a goldsmith in Amsterdam realized

4

that he could, without undue risk, write spurious receipts; that is, receipts for gold over and above the amount of gold in his vault. Since no one would know the difference, he could lend these spurious receipts at interest, taking mortgages or other good securities.

Using other peoples' gold (in his vault) as a pool or partial reserve, the goldsmith added to it as gold was deposited, and paid from it as receipts were brought in, even the spurious receipts, and kept the juggling act going.

The goldsmith knew how much gold was in his vault. Viewing the economy, he could estimate the amount of paper money he could issue and still meet demands for the metal.

Sometimes he might feel that a ten-percent reserve, or even less, was sufficient.

As gold in the vault, the basis of loans, was only a fraction of the receipts (self-created money) the goldsmiths loaned at interest, this was called:

"A FRACTIONAL RESERVE SYSTEM."

The goldsmith was safe. If a loan was not paid, the mortgaged property was sold for enough to redeem the spurious receipts.

The goldsmiths' exorbitant interest charges stripped the earnings and savings from those forced to borrow.

This was the prevailing monetary system in England when the colonization of America began.

CHAPTER 2

Colonization of America: the Search for Economic Freedom

The fearful shadow of despotism lay over England; the despotism of a ruler who proclaimed himself divinely ordained. The few lived in opulence and splendor at the expense of millions who lived in abject poverty. Life itself for most was brutal. A laborer leaving his work and wandering afield would be hanged, without trial, to the nearest tree.[1] Yet in all that darkness a ferment was working in the minds of the masses.

A new world had been discovered across the sea, and eyes that carried for the first time a ray of hope, turned toward it. There one could be his own master. Gradually there evolved the idea of sovereignty of the people — the modern world's idea of representative government.

The trip across the Atlantic was not an easy one. Claude Van Tyne, in the *Causes of the War of Independence,* tells many details . . . "the terrible misery, the stench, fumes, horror . . . sickness, dysentary, scurvy, mouth rot . . . water tasted like ink, biscuits that had to be broken with an axe. Out of one ship that sailed with 150 aboard, 130 died and were thrown into the sea."[2] Still they came — those who braved death in search of freedom.

Three thousand miles of stormy, pirate-infested sea they put between the despots and themselves. They landed and spread out through the new world — but they were not free. They were still chained by the English monetary system. Almost as fast as gold and silver coins drifted into the Colonies, the coins were collected by agents of the overlords and shipped back to London.

At first the lack of money gave no great concern. The government published a priced list of most farm produce, and early trade was effected by barter; chickens, eggs and butter being swapped for shoes, and venison to the tailor for a coat. But soon the population grew too numerous, too widespread and too differentiated for so archaic a system. Stagnation set in. There was frustration and confusion.

The Evolution of a Perfect Money: The Massachusetts Note of 1692

On October 19, 1652, the province of Massachusetts, without authority from the Crown, opened a mint and struck the first Colonial coin — the silver pinetree shilling.[3] There was no real improvement, for these silver shillings too were carried to London and melted down. Frustration and confusion increased. "Colonial trade was cramped into smaller and smaller limits, and the marts and profits of America were transferred to London."[4]

In February 1690, Massachusetts issued its own paper money (notes). At first, these were just promises to pay, but on July 2, 1692, the notes were made full legal tender.[5]

This was freedom indeed. The economic shackles and contrived poverty which had come down through the ages, had been, for this Colony, cast off.

The Massachusetts notes were made full legal tender for

8

all debts, public and private. They were used to pay public expenses, to finance public works, and to lend to its citizens for long periods of time at low interest. The interest from these borrowers was paid into the treasury of the colony and constituted a public revenue which reduced taxes. The colony, itself, paid no interest to anyone. Other colonies also issued notes and there followed a period of unrivaled prosperity.

History goes on to tell how this simple, wonderful plan was brought to an end.

The Bank of England

In England, 1694, William III, needing money to carry on his war with France, gave to one William Patterson and his associates, in return for a loan, a charter to establish a private bank which they called the Bank of England. The king ordered goldsmiths in the London area to stop issuing their receipts, and gave to this Commercial Bank the priceless monopoly of issuing paper money and lending it at interest.

Having taken over London's monetary system, the bankers looked longingly upon the growing prosperity of the Colonies, determined to control the issue of their money also. They used the Board of Trade as their front and acted through Parliament.

In 1720 every Colonial Royal Governor was instructed to curtail the issue of money.[6] The colonists persisted in their Colonial Bills of Credit and prosperity remained high. The Royal Governors were then ordered to destroy the monetary issue of the colonists without regard to consequences.

In 1742 Governor Shirley tricked the Colonial Assembly into passing the ''Equity Act,'' an act containing a clause which read "If they (the Colonial Bills of Credit) depreciated, allowances shall be made accordingly." This comparison of the notes with gold all but demonetized them.[7] Shirley also, by threats, forced the colonists to retire issue after issue of their notes and to refuse notes from other colonies. This resulted in a depression. Prices fell. Trade all but ceased. The Resumption Act (the return to specie) for the Colonies was approved by the King on June 28, 1749. Taxes and other debts were demanded in gold and silver coins. Insiders who knew the blow was coming had hoarded coin against that day. Others could not get coins. The results were disastrous.

"Ruin stalked in every home; the people could not pay their taxes, and were obliged to see their property seized by the sheriff and sold for one-tenth of its previous value." "Every sort of injustice was committed under cover of law."[8] The officials and the favored few became rich.

There followed violence, counterfeiting, defiance of law, and riots.

On April 24, 1751, the Colonial Assembly, in an attempt to have their notes, and at the same time placate the Crown, passed a bill authorizing the issue of interest-bearing notes — to be used as money — the first step on the road to perdition. Perfect money was a thing of the past. But even this concession was not enough. As soon as the issue of these notes became known in London, they, too were ordered stopped.

Benjamin Franklin went to London and attempted to have this order repealed. In a letter to Joseph Galloway, June 13, 1767, he described England's fatal mistake; how in the House of Commons, when the Chancellor of the Exchequer had gone through his proposed revenue from the colonies (duties on glass and the like), Granville, Past Prime Minister, arose and undervaluing all these revenues as trifles said:

"I will tell the honorable gentlemen of a revenue that will produce something valuable in America: make paper money for the colonies, issue it upon loan there, take the interest and apply it as you think proper."[9]

This book will show that this is exactly the way those who control the Federal Reserve System and the Commercial banks prey upon the American people today.

Franklin's appeal fell on deaf ears. The English Government's decree was final. It implemented the Bank of England's determination to own and control the money the colonists used, and to enslave them in debt. Later, Benjamin Franklin wrote: "The colonies would gladly have borne the little tax on tea and other matters, had it not been that England took away from the colonies their money which created unemployment and dissatisfaction."[10]

This was putting it mildly. Del Mar, in his *History of Money,* states: "When in 1774, the Act was promulgated which required a stamp to be placed upon every instrument of commerce, and thus threatened to suppress or defeat the restoration of the paper money system which was at that time being sought, the bitterness of the colonists grew to frenzy and resulted in those acts of resistance to the Crown which have been dignified by the names of the 'battles' of Lexington and Concord. The Crown could have forgiven this but not what followed."

Less than a fortnight later, the Massachusetts Committee of Safety passed a resolution honoring paper money from neighboring colonies and two days later empowered its treasurer to issue interest-bearing bills of credit and pass them into circulation.

"The Congress of all the colonies met June 10, 1775, and on June 22 it resolved to emit $2,000,000 in bills of credit for which redemption the faith of the United Colonies

11

was pledged.''[11]

''Coming as this did during the Crown's efforts to suppress American issue of paper money, it constituted an act of defiance and contempt. The Crown's only course was to punish, if possible, these acts of open rebellion. There was but one course for the colonies — to stand by their monetary system. Thus the Bills of Credit which historians with ignorance or prejudice have belittled as instruments of reckless financial policy, were really the standards of the Revolution. They were more than this; they were the Revolution itself.''[12]

During the Revolutionary War, the Colonial Congress continued to issue paper money. The circumstances are worthy of notice.

The Colonial Congress had no authority from England to issue notes; to force their acceptance, or to guard against counterfeit notes. It could not prevent the various colonies from issuing their own notes in any amount they pleased; it could collect no taxes; it represented thirteen weak colonies contending with the strongest power on earth. Yet the notes remained at par with gold until severe military reverses in 1778, and until the English Generals Howe and Clinton brought in ships with bales of counterfeit colonial notes, and, with the help of Tories, passed them into circulation.[13]

Through the long years of Revolutionary War and through the years of debate that followed, the people's control of their money was uppermost in the minds of the great patriots of the time. That provision was brought up year after year, over and over again in various proposals for the Articles of Confederation from 1776 onward.[14]

The Constitutional Convention

The war came to an end at last, and a convention was being held for the purpose of writing a constitution and

12

forming a union. The goal seemed in a fair way of being achieved. There was, however, a stumbling block. Financiers of New York in league with European bankers had their eyes on the prize — the new nation's purse.

Alexander Hamilton belonged to this group. He was not wealthy himself, but through his marriage, associated with those of great wealth. Hamilton was a banker. He had, in 1784, organized the Bank of New York.[15]

At the Constitutional Convention, Hamilton stood at the head of the delegates from the colony of New York. Although not recognized as such at the time, Hamilton came as a lobbyist for the bankers.

For our purpose it is important that we look closely at this man. What did he want? What did he do? Read the story of Alexander Hamilton in the *Encyclopedia Britannica,* or in almost any American history book.

After trying unsuccessfully to convert individual delegates to his way of thinking, he made an imperious and impassionate speech, urging that the Convention provide that the President of the United States and the Senators be chosen from among the wealthiest men only; that they should hold office for life; that the President should have absolute veto power over all legislation, and should appoint governors of the various states — just as the king of England had appointed his favorites to be the Royal Governors of the Colonies.

When the other delegates would not agree, Hamilton quit the Convention. For a time New York was not represented and the Convention marked time.

Eventually Hamilton returned. He objected to the Bill of Rights, but when Virginia would not yield, he accepted this.

Evidently, Hamilton and his associates had concocted a scheme which would give them their way. For now, seemingly out of character, but actually the same, he ". . . begged each member present to sign the completed document, no matter whether he fully approved of it or not.''[16] The *Constitution* was adopted March 4, 1789. This, the noblest statement of fundamental civil laws ever penned, suffered from serious omissions.

1. There was failure to provide for government payment of all election expenses of government officials. (Under the original rules this would, even now, be a trifle.).

2. There was failure to insist upon faithfulness and absolute integrity of public officials. Where official influence could be involved, there should have been a provision making mandatory a heavy fine and prison sentence for both giver and taker of favor or money — call it bribe or not. The reason for these omissions is easily understood. Most of the signers were honest, patriotic men. It could never have occurred to them that there would come men who loved themselves more than they loved their country; that there would come a time when bribery of public officials and their handing out of special privileges would be the order of the day.

The Turning Point

The *Constitution* was adopted in 1789. It provided in Article I, Section 8, paragraph 5, that ''Congress shall have the power to coin money and regulate the value thereof, and of foreign coin.'' (Foreign coin was legal tender along with our money for a period of 64 years after establishment of our mint.)

The New World was free, but not for long. Hamilton secured the appointment of Secretary of the Treasury. Defying the *Constitution,* the adoption of which he had just urged, and striking straight for his clients' control of the nation's money, he introduced into the House of Representatives a report which would charter a private bank for those wealthy men. There were already three banks operating in the nation. Not one of these would do. Hamilton wanted his own.

The bank he proposed would have the right to issue paper bank notes for use as money and the rights to charge interest on these. The bank would act as the government's tax depository. It would be tax free. The government would be required to assume responsibility for the bank's transactions.

Alexander Hamilton used every wile and trick at his disposal to press for adoption of this report. First of all, he called the bank ''The United States Bank,'' as if it belonged to all the people. It was, in fact, not a central bank as we know them, but a private bank, run for private profit. Hamilton introduced the idea that the government could not be trusted to use its power to issue its own money — that they would issue too much. Yet, when this idea was used against the idea of allowing private bankers to print their own notes, Hamilton brushed it aside by saying this predisposed mismanagement. He also said the bank was but a temporary expedient for twenty years.[17]

A tug of war followed. Thomas Jefferson, who had devised the decimal system to be used in American money, led the fight against the scheme. Jefferson believed that the welfare of the whole, and not the enrichment of any favored group, should be the single role of government. With all the energy he could command he contended that the ownership and control of the nation's money should reside in Congress — that is, with all the people.

The bankers whipped up smear campaigns against those who opposed them. Abuse, intrigue and deceit were used as they sought to secure for themselves control of the government and its people by issuing and controlling the money they used.

The bankers had their way. Jefferson told how members of Congress were bribed by being allowed to profit from the scheme. They gave Hamilton's clients a charter to establish the bank.

This first "United States" bank opened its doors in December 1791. The capital was $10 million, mostly in privately owned government bonds. There were perhaps $400 thousand in cash. The Federal government supplied an additional $2 million in government bonds. The bank was authorized to issue notes on these $2 million bonds (to pay for them), to issue other notes to be loaned at interest, and to accept deposits. The bank's notes were accepted in payment for all debts due the United States, and passed as equal in value to gold.

The bankers had succeeded in usurping the right to make paper money to lend to the people at interest, just as George III and his bankers had proposed to do.

Thus, instead of the new government providing money on equal terms to all citizens, it gave the issue and control of the nation's money and profits from its interest to the financiers who established the first United States Bank.

"Never was a great historic event followed by a more feeble sequel. A nation arises to claim for itself liberty and sovereignty. It gains both of these by an immense sacrifice of blood and treasure. Then, when victory is gained and secure, it hands the nation's credit — that is to say, a national treasure, over to private individuals to do as they please with."[17]

Let us look for a moment at the methods used by Hamilton to operate the office of Secretary of the Treasury, remembering all the while that this is recalled solely for an insight into the way those who control money confuse, dupe, and exploit the American people in our own day.

In one of his letters to Albert Gallatin, then Secretary of the Treasury, 1802, Thomas Jefferson wrote:

"Hamilton . . . in order that he might have the entire government of his machine determined so to complicate it that neither the President or Congress should be able to understand it or control him. . . . He gave to the debt . . . in funding it, the most artificial and mysterious form he could devise. He then moulded up his appropriations of a number of scraps and remnants, many of which were nothing at all, and applied them to different objects until the whole system was involved in an impenetrable fog; and while he was giving himself the air of providing for the payment of the debt, he left himself free to add to it continually, as he did in fact instead of paying it."[18]

Thomas Jefferson continued to speak out for public ownership of the nation's monetary and credit system. In a letter to Albert Gallatin he said:

"If the American people allow the banks to control the issuance of their currency, first by inflation, and then by deflation, the banks and corporations that will grow up around them will deprive people of all property until their children will wake up homeless on the continent their father occupied. The issuing power of money should be taken from the banks and restored to Congress and the people to whom it belongs."[19]

Those early patriots passed from the scene.

Andrew Jackson was elected President. He saw the evils of debt and of private control of the nation's money. In 1835 he announced that the public debt had been paid in full. The next year the charter of the Second United States Bank expired. Jackson vetoed a bill to renew its charter, and ordered government funds withdrawn.

17

Unfortunately Jackson did not give the control of the nation's money to Congress, nor did he formulate a rational plan for it. There followed a chaotic banking system in which many banks made paper money and loaned it at interest to the government and to private borrowers.

CHAPTER 3

The United States Note

The scene shifts to the early days of the Civil War. Men and supplies were desperately needed to equip and mobilize the Union Army. The treasury was empty. Payment of specie (gold and silver coins) had been suspended.

The government had no tokens of indebtedness — that is, no bank notes to give to suppliers in exchange for their goods and services.

Lincoln applied to the bankers for a loan.

There were at that time about 1600 banks chartered in 29 states, together issuing 7,000 different kinds of bank notes. To lend their bank notes (which in reality were nothing but their promises to pay) and to provide bank credit (which was but entries in their ledgers), the bankers, in the nation's hour of need, demanded 28 percent yearly interest.[1]

Lincoln would not yield to the banker's demands. Instead, he persuaded Congress to pass the Act of July 17, 1861, allowing the United States government to print its own notes and pass them into circulation.[2]

The government was thus able to buy all necessary

goods and to obtain all needed services, using its own credit instead of paying the bankers to use bank credit.

QUESTION: Why "notes" instead of just printing dollars?

ANSWER: Because these notes were obligations of the United States government — promises to eventually pay for the goods and services the government would buy on credit. On each note was printed the exact amount of dollars the government owed its bearer.

There was no gold or bond "reserve" behind these notes, and none were needed. The notes themselves were the government's written promise to pay. They were authorized by the Constitution and were backed by the wealth, strength and integrity of the nation.

Still, there were those who raised objections, and the first notes were printed as "Demand Notes." A typical one carried the words: "The United States promises to pay the bearer five dollars on demand." The first issue was sixty million dollars in $5, $10 and $20 denominations.

The "demand" feature implies that the government would exchange gold for the notes. The people knew that the government could not do that. There was no reason to worry about that, however, nor was there reason why the government should pay interest upon the notes, as would have been the case had its creditors been obliged to wait for some distant due date, for the notes themselves passed as money.

The notes were enthusiastically accepted at face value.

As the notes were of small denominations, they were convenient for use in trade. The same day a soldier was paid with them, he could use them to buy provisions for his family. The grocer, in turn, could pay his rent; the landlord his doctor; the doctor a debt, and so on. Finally the notes, relatively a few at a time, were tendered to the government in payment of taxes. By accepting the notes for taxes, the government paid for those goods and services it had bought earlier. In the last analysis this is the only way any government can pay its debts.

The wonderful thing attending the government's issue of its own notes was that all this took place without a middle man. There was no cost, save the small cost of printing. Furthermore at the redemption of the notes, the exact debt was paid and no more. No extra taxes had to be collected to pay a profit to the bankers. The notes helped Lincoln save the Union.

Lincoln gave a Colonel Dick Taylor credit for the idea. In a letter to him, Lincoln said, ". . . But we finally accomplished it and gave to the people of this Republic the greatest blessing they ever had — their own paper to pay their own debts."[3]

Lincoln had taken the first great step.

Next he presented to Congress a bill to make the notes full legal tender. The bill passed in the House, but was held up in the Senate while financiers sought to regain their hold on the nation's monetary system.[4]

Bankers from New York, Boston and Philadelphia hurried to Washington, organized their forces in a formal manner, and invited the Finance Committee of the Senate and the Committee of Ways and Means of the House to meet with them in the office of the Secretary of the Treasury of the United States on January 11, 1862. Thus brazenly these men injected their own personal interest into national affairs, as if they should, by Divine Right, hold the nation's purse.

The bankers stayed on in Washington conferring with Secretary of the Treasury, Chase. As an entering wedge they held that they should not be required to accept the

21

government notes as payment of interest on ''money'' they had loaned the government.[5]

When Lincoln's bill came from Congress, it provided for a ''Legal Tender Note,'' but with a damaging exception. This note bore on the obverse: ''The United States will pay the bearer One Dollar at the Treasury in New York,'' and on the reverse was printed: ''This note is legal tender, for all debts public and private, except duties on imports and interests on the public debt, and is receivable in payment of all loans made to the United States.''[6] The bill was signed February 25, 1862.

The provision that the interest on government bonds could not be paid with the notes, but that the bond itself could be paid with them may seem a strange compromise — strange, that is, until it is remembered that the government was paying the interest annually while payment of the bonds was some years away. The financiers through their influence in the Senate could change this concession before payment of the bonds was due. That is what happened.

The exception, printed on the note, had the effect the bankers desired. It showed that the notes were not a complete money. Their value, as compared to gold, quickly fell.

Bankers, today, would have us believe that the decline in value of the notes was due to the fact that the government issued them — that they were inflationary.

Congressman Wright Patman, then Chairman of the House Committee on Banking and Currency, said: ''It is a fallacy to think, as many do, that the greenback was inflationary. In the only sense that matters, the relative or comparative sense, they were not. That is, $450 millions in greenbacks is no more or less inflationary than $450 millions in bank deposits, or any other bank money created to pay for $450 millions in interest-bearing bonds.''[7]

Pressure against the notes continued as the financiers

marshaled their nationwide campaign.

The *Hazard Circular,* distributed to bankers in 1862, declared: "The great debt the capitalists will see to is made out of the Civil War by opposing the government issue of money, must be used as a measure to control the value of money. To provide the people with money will seriously affect your profits as bankers and lenders."[8]

Secretary of the Treasury, Chase, now joined the bankers in their demand that the power to issue the nation's money be returned to them.

Day after day these men subjected Lincoln to all possible pressure. Lincoln spoke of his utter weariness: "They persist, they have argued me almost blind — I am worse off than St. Paul. He was in a strait between two, I am in a strait between twenty and they are bankers and financiers."[9]

Weary, preoccupied with the war, subjected to vicious abuse and ridicule, his notes reduced in value by their new wording, Lincoln could not resist.

In 1863 Congress passed a law chartering a new privately owned banking system, The National Banks, and gave it power to issue money. The government was again forced to issue bonds — and sell them $1 in bonds for $1 of the depreciated Legal Tender Note.

The following year Congress freed National Banks from most taxes.[10]

Robert Friedberg, in his *Paper Money of the United States,* lists 14,348 National banks chartered between 1863 and 1929, all of which could print money.

At the end of the Civil War, Lincoln was assassinated.

As the purpose of this chapter is to trace the development of Lincoln's note, one might think that upon the return to private hands of the power to issue the nation's money, the depression of the notes' value, and the death of the notes' sponsor, the discussion of the note should end.

There were, however, other significant turns in the note's devious course to maturity — and their ultimate suppression.

There is also a lesson to be learned.

As the value of the note sank lower, down to 35¢ on the dollar, the bankers bought most of them. Why?

Because the United States (one dollar) note, while worth only 35¢, would buy a one dollar government bond. Not only did the bankers collect interest on these bonds, but using the bond as collateral, they could, by law, print 90 percent of the par or market value of the bonds (whichever sum was smaller) of their own currency, and lend this on interest.

Firmly in control of the nation's money and credit system, the bankers had nothing to fear. With large holdings of the notes, any advance in the notes' value meant money in their vaults.

The time for payment of the bonds neared. The bankers had agreed that the bonds could be paid with the government's Legal Tender Note — the same notes the bankers had used to pay for the bonds. Were they sincere, or had it all been a trick?

On the 13th of March, 1868, Baron James Rothschild wrote to Mr. Belmont a letter: ". . . warning ruin to those who might oppose the payment of U.S. Bonds in coin, or who might advocate their liquidation in greenbacks."[11]

The financiers needed a man in the White House who would allow this raid on the Treasury. They manipulated the election of Ulysses S. Grant. Del Mar tells the story of intrigue and treachery.[12]

Corruption in government reached a new high. The two really distinguished and honest men in the Cabinet were soon removed. From histories of the time it seems that the passage of any bill the financiers presented to the Congress, the ordering of any act they requested of the administration, the virtual gift of any property of the nation which they coveted, could be obtained. A number of today's great fortunes were founded on these gifts.

The so-called "Credit Strengthening Act" of March 18, 1869, was passed by the newly elected Congress and signed by President Grant. The words on the legal tender note reading, ". . . and is receivable in payment of all loans made to the United States" were dropped. The Act provided that United States bonds, purchased with the depreciated notes (worth as low as 35¢ on the dollar), should be paid dollar for dollar in gold. From 1869 onward the notes bore the name, United States Note.

On "Black Friday," September 24, 1869, Jay Gould and John Fisk, Jr., aided by inside information from the Administration, bought up a controlling part of the available supply of the nation's gold, and withdrew it from circulation.

This caused an enormous drop in the money supply — not only of gold, but also of bank notes based on gold. Debtors with notes and mortgages falling due could not get money to pay. A farmer may have had great wealth in cattle, grain and land, but the banker's debt could not be settled with these. The bankers demanded payment in their own notes and coin which had been withdrawn from circulation.

Gold rose in price to $162.5 an ounce. Debtors' properties were taken from them at a small fraction of their real value. A severe panic ensued. This caused delay in redemption of the bonds. The nation's monetary policy remained confused. Debtors wanted a paper money. The bankers contended for a money based on gold. The government gave way to the bankers and agreed to keep a reserve of $100 million in gold coins and bullion in the treasury.

An Act of Congress on February 28, 1878, authorized

the production of Silver Certificates. An Act of May 3, 1878, fixed the amount of United States Notes that must be maintained, outstanding, to $346,681,016.

Resumption of specie payment, and redemption of notes and bonds with gold were resumed January 1, 1879. The Treasury paid European bankers some $500 million in gold, above what these bankers had paid for the bonds.

Financiers began manipulation of the Treasury's gold reserve. J.P. Morgan, the nation's leading banker, acting for the Rothschilds, was one of the most active. Tens of millions of dollars in depreciated paper notes, bought at reduced prices, were brought to the Treasury, and upon demand redeemed, at their printed face value, with gold. The financiers would demand that the Treasury replenish its reserve by buying the gold back from them with paper notes at the notes' depressed value.

This exchange of notes for gold and then gold for notes was done by back and forth shifting of labels of ownership in the Treasury vault, all on the same gold. President Cleveland finally stopped the practice.

There were gold money and gold certificates (issued for general circulation in 1882), and then the money of lesser esteem, silver and silver certificates, United States Notes, and hundreds of different kinds of National Bank Notes.

In all this monetary confusion the national economy reached a low point. These were the days of the Cleveland panic; of William Jennings Bryan's cry that mankind was crucified on a cross of gold. The nation was young then. There were few people. The land was overflowing with natural resources. There was but one explanation for those years of poverty and want — and that was the private control of the people's medium of exchange — its manipulation for bankers personal gain.

In 1900 Congress passed a law making the United States

gold dollar the nation's unit of value, and directed that all our money be kept at par with it.

The United States Note, which, within Lincoln's concept contained the key to prosperity, still bore the damaging exceptions and the obligation.

There was sore need for reform of the nation's monetary system — a need to widen its control through a takeover by Congress (all the people), not for what followed.

CHAPTER 4

Founders of Our Present Monetary System

The year 1907 was a lean one. The evils inherent in private control of the nation's monetary system had once more come to a head. The Standard Oil group, owners of "Amalgamated Copper," had set about breaking one Mr. Heinze, central figure in the rival "Union Copper Company." They drove down the price of that company's stock — from 60 to 10. There was uneasiness, and depositors began withdrawing money from banks in which Heinze was heavily involved. The trouble crystalized when Morgan publicly declared that one of these, the Knickerbocker Trust Company, was the weak point.

With the crash of this bank, many others went down. Millions of dollars went into lock boxes. Banks called their loans — and debtors had no money to pay. A severe depression followed. Millions of people were sold out and rendered homeless. There was no government help in those days. The destitute and hungry shifted for themselves. Money in circulation was practically non-existent. Many business concerns printed their IOU's on small bits of paper and exchanged these for raw materials and for the labor of their workers. These "tokens" passed from hand to hand as a medium of exchange.[1]

Mr. Morgan reappeared. He raised funds here and abroad and, through President Theodore Roosevelt, secured $35 million from the U.S. Treasury. He saved the last Heinze bank: the Trust Company of America. His price was the right to purchase, below value, the bank's controlling stock in the Tennessee Coal and Iron Company (Birmingham, Alabama). Its potential value was enormous. Morgan's agent in Washington persuaded the President that economic conditions made it necessary to allow Morgan to add this company to his own United States Steel Company — notwithstanding anti-trust laws.[2]

Mr. Morgan then presented his plan. It was an extension of the "token" idea. In the name of the New York Banker's Clearing House Association he secured the President's approval to print and issue over $200 million in Clearing House Certificates secured solely by the banker's promise to pay. In a slightly different form the certificates were paid out at the teller's windows and functioned as money. The depression was brought under control.

Woodrow Wilson, historian and educator, was the most prominent man in his field. In *A History of the American People,* 1902, he had extolled Lincoln's "greenbacks." He now, unmindful of Morgan's earlier raids on the Treasury; unmindful of the causes of the depression; unmindful of Morgan's price for help; and apparently unable to distinguish between Lincoln's simple faith and the motives of those who issued the Clearing House certificates, declared: "All this trouble could be averted if we appointed a committee of six or seven public-spirited men like J.P. Morgan to handle the affairs of our country."

These events, apparently so lacking in significance, changed the history of the world. Woodrow Wilson had written a number of political articles that had attracted the common man's attention with their high moral tone. Here, in his adoration of Morgan, he attracted the attention of those of great wealth — such a man could be useful. Here, too, in the gift to a privately owned clearing house of the right to create paper money by a line in a ledger and pass it on to private banks, was the inception of the Federal Reserve System.

The bankers saw the limitless possibilities of the scheme. From that time onward, never wavering, they exerted all possible pressure toward the goal of making this innovation a permanent policy of the government. First, they secured passage of the Aldrich-Vreeland Act of 1908. This was essentially a continuation of the Clearing House scheme, to serve until they could get the bill they wanted.

There were other steps — several of them, on the way to their goal.

First, it was necessary to create a popular demand for change in the monetary system. Article after article inspired by the bankers appeared in the press. The seed fell on fertile soil. Gradually there spread a clamor for reform.

The Aldrich Committee

In 1908, Congress authorized a National Monetary Commission to study the problem. Senator Nelson Aldrich secured the position of chairman. This was not an auspicious beginning. Aldrich, through his extensive personal fortune and his intimate connections with powerful financial groups, had become a leader in the Senate. He had used this position to sponsor a series of laws favorable to moneyed interests.

Instead of going to the *Constitution* for the answer, the Commission went to Europe. When they returned, the only

31

tangible results for the $300,000 expenditure were more than twenty massive volumes on European banking. Typical of these works is the thousand-page history of the *Reichsbank,* the central bank which controlled money and credit in Germany, and whose principal stockholders were members of the Warburg family. Aldrich made no announcement. Instead, he conferred with Wall Street bankers.

Next came real help. Paul Warburg, a German financier, arrived in America — ostensibly as a partner in the Rothschild dominated bank of Kuhn, Loeb and Company in New York.

Instead of staying at his desk he spent much of his time writing and lecturing on money and banking and advocating reform of the American system. These activities brought him recognition as an expert in his field; and his seeming passionate desire to clip the bankers' wings, prepared the people's minds for what followed.

(Woodrow Wilson was tendered the nomination of Governor of New Jersey in September 1910.)

The Bankers Decide Our Future

On the night of November 22, 1910, Senator Aldrich slipped out of New York to board a train in Hoboken, New Jersey. With Senator Aldrich was A.P. Andrews, professional economist and Assistant Secretary of the Treasury, who had traveled with Aldrich to Europe. Through the darkness came also Frank Vanderlip, President of the National Bank of New York City; Harry P. Davidson, senior partner of J.P. Morgan Company; Charles D. Norton, President of Morgan's First National Bank of New York; Paul Warburg, partner of the banking house of Kuhn, Loeb and Company of New York; and lastly Benjamin Strong of J.P.

Morgan Company. These men came separately, and in silence. The train, with curtains drawn, rolled out of the yard.

Where were they going? Why the secrecy? Their destination was J.P. Morgan's estate at the ''Millionaires' Club'' at Jekyll's Island, Georgia. They went to write a new monetary bill for Senator Aldrich to present to Congress.

The bankers remained at Jekyll's Island for nine days. All had a hand in writing the bill, but Paul Warburg was its chief architect. The first serious break in the bankers' accord came when Senator Aldrich wished to present the bill to Congress as ''The Aldrich Plan.''

Warburg argued in vain that the use of the Aldrich name would disclose the fact that the bill represented the great Wall Street interests — that it would make the bill hard, if not impossible, to pass. Aldrich and the others could not be convinced. It was decided that the bill should be presented as ''The Aldrich Plan.''

The bankers returned. Their plan had been perfected. The next problem was to sell it to the American people. The national banks contributed five million dollars for propaganda. The great universities to which the financiers contributed served as centers from which to mislead the nation.

Congressman Patman's *A Primer on Money,* states: ''The main reform proposed was a central bank with power to regulate. The central bank was to be privately owned and privately controlled.''[3]

A presidential election was just ahead. The Republican Party incorporated the Aldrich Plan into its platform and pledged to enact it into law.

It happened, however, that an independent investigation by the House of Representatives unearthed the fact that a few Wall Street tycoons controlled almost all the financial power of the nation.

Public aversion to the Aldrich Plan set in. There persisted, however, a wide public demand for a Central Authority to regulate all banks and to maintain reserves for them, but with this demand there was now the determination that all should be under the ownership and control of the United States Government.

If there is one thing that time has taught, it is that powerful financiers with their army of high-paid advisers, shrewd lawyers, and lobbyists never give up. If the Republicans couldn't pass the bill as the Aldrich Plan, could it be renamed "The Federal Reserve Act" — a name suggesting that it is part of the government, carry suggestions of fair play which could later be eliminated, and be passed into law by the Democrats?

Yes, it could!

Woodrow Wilson was a minister's son, an educator, a man the people trusted, one who had spoken so idealistically of the people's ownership of their monetary system; yet one already in the bankers' camp, and beholden to them. Here was the man.

The bankers checked again. Frank Vanderlip, who had helped write the Aldrich Plan, invited Wilson to luncheon with James Stillman, President of the National City Bank. Wilson was nominated.

The bankers couldn't lose. The Republicans carried the bill as the Aldrich Plan; the Democrats carried it as the "Federal Reserve Act."

Woodrow Wilson promised the people a money and credit system free from Wall Street influence. He was elected President of the United States in 1912.

Wilson's campaign had been almost entirely financed by Cleveland H. Dodge of Kuhn, Loeb's National Bank; Jacob Schiff, senior partner in Loeb's National Bank; Henry Morganthau, Sr.; Bernard Baruch; and Samuel Untermyer.

34

An intimate associate of these bankers, Edward House, was assigned to Wilson as ''Advisor.'' He stood always by Wilson's side and seemed to direct every important move of that administration.

The Federal Reserve Act was passed into law December 23, 1913, under pressure of adjournment. It was signed into law immediately.

The details of all this may be read in H.S. Keenan's *The Federal Reserve Banks.*[4]

CHAPTER 5

The Federal Reserve Act of 1913[1]

This Act was introduced:

"To provide for the establishment of Federal Reserve Banks, to furnish an electric currency, to afford means of rediscounting commercial paper, to establish a more effective supervision of banking in the United States, and for other purposes."

These principles were so necessary and so laudible. But just how would they be accomplished? Who would administer the system and reap its benefits — the people or the bankers? What were the "other purposes"? The Act is a masterpiece of dissimulation.

Question of Ownership

If, as claimed, the Federal Reserve was to be the nation's central bank, operated for the benefit of all its people, the Treasury should have provided money to start operation.

But no! The bankers insisted that it be financed by sales of Federal Reserve stock to commercial banks — six percent

37

of each commercial banks' capital. (This was reduced to three percent.)

Objections to commercial bank ownership, implied by ownership of "stock," were met by the provision that this stock would not command dividends, but six percent annual interest. Quieting too, was the provision that the stock could not be transferred; and that in case of repeal of the Act, the stock, together with the Federal Reserve system assets would pass to the United States Government upon payment to the member commercial banks of the amount they advanced, together with any interest due.

Then came the real use of the word stock — the stock of proprietorship, the right to vote, the right to control. Not all stock was to carry this right — only the stock owned by the banks. The great banks were given the highest voice.

There was a provision that if the banks did not subscribe all the stock, the United States Government (and others) could buy the remainder. Such stock, however, was to have no voting right.

A question arises. If the government owned the system, just why should it buy stock? And again, just why should that particular stock be denied a voice in management?

The banks took all the "stock" that was issued.

Management — Control

Much of the Federal Reserve Act was devoted to organization. It provided for a monetary system to be implemented and administered by a central board, with offices in Washington, operating twelve Regional Federal Reserve banks scattered throughout the nation. The central board was to be composed of seven directors, appointed by the United States President, with Senate approval, for a term of ten years. At first, these directors were staggered so that the term of one expired every two years. Each incoming President appoints one of these as chairman. The Secretary of the Treasury and the Comptroller of Currency were ex-officio members.

It was claimed by the authors of the Act that the unusually long term of office of Federal Reserve officials would remove these men from political influence. Actually, it removed them from all government control and placed them under the influence of the enormously wealthy and powerful financiers with whom they are often associated and who could give them jobs when their term of office expired.

This tie-in with the financiers is strengthened by another strange provision of the Act. The salaries of the Board, paid from profits which should come to the Treasury, are not paid by the U.S. Treasury. These men are paid by the Regional Reserve Banks, as if they worked for the bankers.

Once the President appoints these men and they are placed in office, they operate the system as they please.

Each of the twelve Federal Reserve Regional Banks are operated by a board composed of nine directors. It is the same story here. Mr. Patman states that: ''Private commercial bankers were given control over these Regional Banks, that is, they were given the privilege of electing two-thirds of the directors and these directors, in turn, selected the president and chief officers of the banks'' *(A Primer on Money,* pp. 58-59).

Chief Function

The chief function of the Federal Reserve was to insure elasticity of money.

This was to be accomplished by discounting their member banks' sound eligible bank paper — thus quickly supplying those banks with needed funds.

Profits

All net profits (after paying for buildings) were to be paid to the United States Treasury. (This proved to be a very disarming provision. It helped to get the Act passed. It was changed six years later.)

Duration

The duration of the Act was set at 20 years.

Right of Repeal

The last paragraph of the Act is the saving one. Section 30 — "THE RIGHT TO AMEND/OR REPEAL THIS ACT IS HEREBY EXPRESSLY RESERVED."

Amendments

In 1914 the long list of banker-inspired amendments began. In order that the reader may see the connection, mention is made of the recessions and depressions, produced by the bankers, which enabled them to extend their grasp.

Profits Go to the Federal Reserve

Amendment: "After all necessary expenses of a Federal Reserve Bank shall have been paid or provided for, the stockholders shall be entitled to receive an annual dividend of six per centum on the paid in capital stock, which dividend shall be cumulative. After the aforesaid dividend claims have been fully met, the net earnings shall be paid into the surplus fund of the Federal Reserve Bank." (U.S.C. Title 12, Sec. 289, as amended by Act of March 3, 1919.)

(40 Stat 1314): June 16, 1933 (48 Stat 163).

Background of the Great Depression

Large government expenditures to finance World War I and post war aid to Europe had placed huge fortunes into the hands of the nation's wealthiest men — those who had created money and loaned it at interest, and those who owned the munition plants and the factories that had supplied the needs of Europe. This expanded production and the jobs scattered money through the nation.

In 1921 there was a tightening of credit by the Federal Reserve and a short recession.

There was then a reversal of policy by the Federal Reserve. There was an outpouring of credit to commercial banks, and a corresponding increase of bank loans to the people.

Those financiers who controlled the daily ups and downs of the Stock Market began to buy more and more stock. Buying from each other they forced stock prices higher and higher: far beyond prices justified by the stock earnings. People who had never owned stock, seeing this rise, ventured in. As prices soared, more and more people poured in their money, and borrowing from banks bought stock on margin as low as ten percent. A spirit of speculation swept through the nation. Real estate prices rose higher and higher, as speculators bought and sold — largely on credit. Fortunes, on paper, were made overnight.

In those rosy days of 1927, financiers decreed and Congress passed a bill extending the Federal Reserve Act of 1913 indefinitely.

All unknown to the average man was the fact that the great financiers — who had planned it all — had, by then, sold their stock to newcomers at the market's inflated prices; and further, after all their holdings were sold, the financiers were selling stock short; that is, they were selling, at the prevailing high prices, stock which they did not have. They did this in anticipation of obtaining the stock at lower prices for later delivery.

There was a veritable frenzy of gambling. The climb in prices reached its height.

The time was ripe. There was a silent change at the core of our economy. Those men who controlled the Federal Reserve System directed it to clamp down on credit, and refuse to discount notes from commercial banks. Buying slowed and the Stock Market faltered. Prices fell somewhat. Stock brokers called for additional money to protect marginal stock. Those people who had borrowed to buy on a thin margin requested more bank loans. The bankers not only refused but called the loans the people did have. There was no cash to pay. Huge blocks of stock were thrown on the market.

The financiers on the inside did not buy. Others could not protect their holdings. October 29, 1929, brought the Stock Market crash. Stock losses between 1929 and 1931 were estimated at $50 billion. All prices plummeted. Postwar prosperity was at an end. The great depression began. Millions of people lost their homes — their all.

The financiers next move was to instruct Congress to force the people to give up their gold.

We were on the gold standard as the great depression began. This fact had not helped. In going off the gold standard, there was no honest reason to take the peoples' gold. With Congress, it was reason enough that the financiers wanted it. Then, as now, the big, international bankers had their puppets in Washington.

In the 72nd *Congressional Record,* 2nd Session, February 22, 1933, page 4700, Senator Elmer Thomas stated: "Any time Wall Street wants a bill passed they send a suggestion down to Washington and we are kept here sometimes until midnight to pass the bill. But if Wall Street is opposed to legislation it cannot be gotten out of committee, and it cannot be gotten before the Senate for consideration, and it has no chance of passing."

On June 5, 1933, Congress passed a law, backed by threats of a heavy fine and a long term in the penitentiary, forcing the owners of gold coin and gold certificates to surrender them to the Treasurer of the United States. Amid great fanfare, the gold was placed in Fort Knox. Since then most of it has drifted out to international bankers. (On an ABC newscast, September 17, 1980, it was stated that in one New York bank vault there is two and a half times as much gold as there is in Fort Knox!)

To relieve the shortage of money, Congress authorized the President to print three billion dollars in United States notes. The President was persuaded by the financiers not to print the notes. They assured him that they were able to supply the money. They didn't.

The Secretary of the Treasury then withdrew the type of bonds upon which the National Banks issued their notes — making it impossible for these banks to increase the money supply. (They hadn't been *used* since 1913.)

In 1933 and 1935, still in the depression, other amendments were demanded, and obtained. One amendment gave authority to vary the reserve requirement percentage for affiliated banks. In 1934, the Federal Reserve was given the power to set the percentage of cash down payments on stock market purchases.

In 1935 an amendment eliminated the Secretary of the Treasury and the Comptroller of Currency from the board. (The financiers wanted full and secret control of the Federal Reserve.) The board was now called The Seven Governors.

Their term of office was extended to 14 years.

In 1935 also, an amendment provided that government securities could be bought and sold only in what bankers called ''The Open Market'' division of the Federal Reserve. This amendment ushered in the change from the declared purpose of the Federal Reserve — the discounting of eligible bank paper — and made the Federal Reserve into an institution for the creation and manipulation of government bonds.

The great depression, precipitated by the Federal Reserve's monetary policies, continued.

During World War I the industrialists and bankers had made great fortunes while the soldiers fought in the trenches for a dollar a day. Later those soldiers were promised a small bonus to be paid years later.

In the depths of the great depression these veterans, who had endured the horrors of war for their country, were unable to find work. Their families were destitute; they themselves penniless, ragged, hungry. Thousands of them gathered in Washington to petition their government for help. They were driven out with bayonets. President Hoover, a millionaire himself, must bear the responsibility for that.

Several years passed. The Federal Reserve continued to withhold money from the nation. The financiers continued to increase their wealth and power. The veterans continued to stand in long lines for free soup. Some sold apples on the streets.

A few in Congress proposed that the bonus to veterans be paid then — for two reasons: One, to help the veterans; and two, in the belief that the release of several billion dollars into cities, towns, villages and farms would raise purchasing power and mitigate the depression.

After long controversy involving several presidential vetoes, the bill was enacted, and the money paid in August

1936.

To those government officials who had voted for the plan, it seemed strange that the payments had no effect on the depression.

Long afterwards it came to light that in June 1936 the Federal Reserve raised the reserve requirements of commercial bank loans in anticipation of the inflationary effect of the soldiers' bonus. (This, despite the fact that 17 percent of the workmen were unemployed.) This act subsequently plunged the economy into the deadening relapse of 1937-38.

The Federal Reserve continued its tight money policy. Individuals and firms were forced into bankruptcy and valuable assets were sold and bought for a small fraction of their real value.

It was the duty of the Federal Reserve to supply an elastic currency. It could have supplied the money in a day — but would not. The officials deliberately withheld money while tens of millions of homes and businesses were foreclosed.

Of course the financiers who made hundreds of millions of dollars do not accept blame for the depression. Nor do the Federal Reserve officials accept blame for allowing it to continue. The following, however, is certain. It was said by Sheldon Emry:

"In 1930 Americans did not lack industrial capacity, fertile farms, land, skilled and willing workers or industrious farm families. It had an extensive and highly efficient transportation system in railroads, road networks, inland and ocean waterways. Communication between region and localities was the best in the world, utilizing telephone, telegraph, radio and well operated government rail service. No war had ravaged the cities, or pestilence weakened the population; no famine stalked the land. The United States of America in 1930 lacked only one thing; an ample supply of money to carry on trade and commerce."[2]

Money was available — Lincoln's note — the best money in the world, costing nothing but the printing, but the bankers objected to its use.

It was not until World War II that money and credit, the life blood of the economy, again flowed freely.

In March 1951, another far-reaching amendment was enacted, the so-called "Accord Agreement." This amendment was obscure, hazy, misunderstood, as these amendments are wont to be. From that date the Federal Reserve claimed complete independence.

The Honorable Wright Patman, in the House of Representatives, July 27, August 2, 3, and 7, 1967, tells how the Federal Reserve System tried to achieve total independence under Presidents Roosevelt and Truman and were rebuffed. Those presidents insisted that interest on government bonds be held at a low rate. Then came President Dwight Eisenhower who, on October 5, 1956, stated: "The Federal Reserve Board is not under my control, and I think it proper that Congress did set it up as an independent agency."

The Federal Reserve Board has, ever since, quoted these words and has defied all interference. Mr. Patman states that during the succeeding 14 years, after Mr. Eisenhower's give-away, the American people paid $211 billion in excess interest charges.

The United States Note (Again)
Its Maturity and Its Passing

Lincoln's notes had been crippled with exceptions and the obligation (promise to pay — as if the notes were not real money). They had been belittled by bankers. They had been relegated to a minor role in our currency by a great outpouring of many other kinds of money. And yet, in their century of service, they had saved the taxpayers many millions of dollars in interest.

In the 1963H issue, the $5 note came into flower. This note carried no exception and no obligation. Each bore the caption: UNITED STATES NOTE, and each bore the simple all-important line: ''This note is legal tender for all debts public and private.'' Each note carried the signature of the U.S. Treasurer and of the Secretary of the Treasury and each bore the Treasury Seal — all notorizing, in effect, the indebtedness of the government to the holder of the note.

This was the nation's own note — totally free (until payment), save for the printing. It showed that the government need not issue United States Bonds and give them to bankers to sweeten the pot for them as they used their credit to issue and control the nation's money. It showed that the nation could use its own credit to issue its own notes — for use as money.

A mature United States note is shown in the upper part of our frontispiece. This is the note advocated in this book.

If the note had been left in circulation it would have, in time, shown us what money should be. Its use would have told us that the United States note, used as the Massachusetts note was used, would free the nation from debt.

The very perfection of the note was its undoing. Its threat to the bankers was short lived. The bankers saw to that.

The total amount of United States notes which must be maintained was fixed by Congressional action. The Act did not specify the amount of each denomination. That was the loophole.

Near the last of October 1968 Secretary of the Treasury Henry Fowler announced that the Treasury would stop printing $5 and $10 United States notes and that in the

47

future it would print only $100 notes. The last delivery of the $100 United States notes was on January 26, 1971.

A Study of the Federal Reserve

The Federal Reserve Act of 1913 contained 27 pages. As we have seen, it was an unclear collection of rules on credit. A flexible currency was to be obtained by discounting sound and eligible commercial bank paper.

Amended and amended and the amendments amended — in total or in part — reaffirmed and changed again, the 1966 edition of the Act, mixed with laws on banking, contained 651 pages of fine print.

I resolved to find out what it said. In the book and on separate paper I crossed out those sections annulled, and added the new ones. Soon the produce became confusing. This was cumulative. Many provisions used code numbers to refer to amendments or laws, not otherwise identified or explained, and not available to me.

I worked for days. By the time I reached the 150th page, the Act had become an absolute maze. I gave up. No man's mind can follow it. No congressman can know what it means or know whether a new amendment, asked for, is necessary. The entire maze seemed irrational *unless it was created for the purpose of obscurity, secrecy and deception.*

A new edition came out in 1971. The Federal Reserve had become the depository and manager of many government agencies. Laws governing the handling of these agencies have been placed in an appendage. The Federal Reserve Act had been reduced to 60 pages by omitting most amendments and replacing them with their numbers.

On page 30, section 12, 3, there are only a few words to the provision:

"PURCHASE AND SALE OF OBLIGATIONS OF

UNITED STATES, COUNTIES, ETC.'' Its amendments were given by numbers only. There were twenty-three of these. If the 1966 edition was an enigma, this one is a vacuum.

Most of the book dealt with organizations, duties, penalties and the like — of both the Federal Reserve banks and their member banks. Here and there are sentences giving the Board of Governors wide latitude, such as the use of their own discretion in forming policies.

Much of the Act was obsolete for it dealt with the discounting of commercial bank paper. (In 1964 Mr. Wright Patman said that the discounting of bank paper hadn't been done in years, that U.S. bonds were used.) *The Federal Reserve,* published by The American Banking Association, Columbia Press, 1974, says that the U.S. government *debt* is sufficient to serve as the basis of our monetary system!

(The stated purpose of the original Act was to rediscount commercial paper. Nothing was said about government debts and bonds. Just how and why were these brought in?)

Evidently government bonds are used in these manipulations — but how? One may read and reread the Act and still not have the slightest idea. It simply does not tell.

Fortunately there was in Congress a very dedicated man who for some 45 years pled the people's cause against the bankers. He was the Honorable Wright Patman, former Chairman of the House Committee on Banking and Currency.

Mr. Patman's notes, written over that long period of time, are published as: *A Primer on Money,* August 5, 1964, and its supplement, *Money Facts,* September 21, 1964. Both are from the Committee on Banking and Currency, 88th Congress, 2nd Session, of and printed by the U.S. Government Printing Office, Washington, D.C.

49

Yet, even from these fine notes, it is difficult for the uninitiated to get a compact, definite picture of the Federal Reserve System and its operation. The notes are, however, invaluable in a further study. They serve as a veritable Rosetta stone in deciphering, not only the Federal Reserve Act, but the Federal Reserve System. The Act, *The Federal Reserve* of the bankers and all associated literature now begin to take on a meaning, and furnish the missing links. The gist and conclusions of the writer's study are set down in the next chapter. They are spelled out and given in some length so there can be no mistake in their meaning.

CHAPTER 6

The Federal Reserve as It Was in 1974

To the Federal Reserve's Board of seven governors, Washington offices, and its 12 regional banks, there have been added the Open Market Committee, Advisory Council and 25 branches.[1]

"The Federal Reserve is a complete money making machine."[2] It may create, or, if it chooses, extinguish billions of dollars in a few seconds. It controls the amount of bank credit and money we use. It has gained control and management of government financing. Through its manipulations, "The government has been reduced to the position of a perpetual borrower at interest from a private monopoly."[3]

The Federal Reserve Open Market Committee is the brains and the chief executive committee of the system.

Federal Reserve Open Market Committee

This committee consists of nineteen members. There are twelve who vote: the seven Federal Reserve governors; the president of the Federal Reserve Regional Bank of New

York, *always;* and four of the other Federal Reserve Regional Bank presidents in yearly rotation. The other seven Regional Bank presidents attend, advise and persuade. The committee is heavily weighted with men who represent those whose private profits depends upon the committee's actions. The committee operates behind closed doors.

This committee has several important functions. An amendment to the Act provides: ''Any bonds, notes, or other obligations, which are direct obligations of the United States or which are fully guaranteed by the United States as to principal and interest may be bought and sold without regard to maturity but only in the open market.'' Federal Reserve Act 1971, Page 30, Sec. 14, 3, b(2). The law also names the twenty dealers who may buy in this market. These dealers are linked to financial institutions. They sell the bonds to other dealers, banks, insurance companies, foundations and the like, and to individuals. The transactions of these dealers buying and selling government securities amounts to some $600 billion a year.

Each week the Secretary of the Treasury prepares a statement of the amount of money the government will need the following week. United States notes and bonds are sold in the open market the following Monday — unless a holiday — then Friday. Treasury bills are auctioned off. Other government securities are sold at a fixed price. On February 2, 1976, the Treasury's refunding operation called for:

1.   The sale of bonds creating $4.2 billion in net ''new money.''

2.   The bill auction of some $7 billion in Treasury notes of three months duration, and the sale of bonds of up to 29.25 year maturity for existing money.

52

We will first consider the creation of the "New Money." This will show how the "old" money to buy the other securities had been created.

The Federal Reserve's Usual Way of Creating Money

When, in long-term government borrowing, there is call for "new money," the Treasury prepares interest bearing bonds (promises to pay) and sends them to the open market. From there they are sent to the Federal Reserve Bank.

The Federal Reserve has no money to purchase these bonds and needs none. The Federal Reserve Bank puts the bonds in its vault and credits the government's account with the amount of the bonds. This is done by simply writing a notation of the transaction in its ledger and entering the credit upon its computer. The very act of entering the credit creates the money.

Such statements have been verified many times. When Marriner Eccles, the Chairman of the Federal Reserve Board, was testifying before the House Banking and Currency Committee, September 30, 1941, Congressman Patman asked:

"Mr. Eccles, how did you get the money to buy these two billion dollars of government bonds?"

Mr. Eccles: "We created it."

Mr. Patman: "Out of what?"

Mr. Eccles: "Out of the right to create credit money."

In *The Primer,* on page 38, Mr. Patman tells that upon hearing that Federal Reserve Banks hold a large amount of cash, he went to two of its regional banks. He asked to see their bonds. He was led into vaults and shown great piles of government bonds upon which the people are taxed for interest. Mr. Patman then asked to see their cash. The bank officials seemed confused. When Mr. Patman repeated the request, they showed him some ledgers and blank checks.[4]

Mr. Patman warns us to remember that:

"The cash, in truth, does not exist and never has existed. What we call 'cash reserves' are simply bookkeeping credits entered upon the ledgers of the Federal Reserve Banks. These credits are created by the Federal Reserve Banks and then passed along through the banking system."

To make clear the way this government credit is converted into commercial bank reserve, upon which these banks base their loans, and to make clear the method of distribution of this new "reserve" among commercial banks, we state: (Section 15, p. 32, Federal Reserve Act, 1971), that the United States Treasury has an account in the Federal Reserve Bank just as an individual has in a commercial bank and that "disbursement may be made by checks drawn against such accounts," the Act, p. 32, Sec. 15, 1.

In the present case the Treasury has just sold through the open market to the Federal Reserve $4.2 billion of U.S. Bonds, and has received upon the Federal Reserve books and computer an additional credit (a deposit) to its account.

Let us now say that the Treasury, in paying a charge for armaments, has written a check for $3 billion against this deposit. The check is deposited by the armament factory in, say, the Chase Manhattan Bank. This bank credits the armament corporation account with that amount, and sends the check to the Federal Reserve bank for payment. The Federal Reserve stamps the check "Paid" and, debiting the Treasury's account, credits the account to the Chase Manhattan.

This credit (to the account of the Chase Manhattan Bank on the Federal Reserve computers), is the "Reserve" upon which the Chase Manhattan Bank may base its fractional reserve loans!

54

The Chase Manhattan makes loans (several times the amount of the reserve), and the borrowers, having received book entries in their accounts in the Chase Manhattan, write checks against it. Some of these checks will be deposited in the Chase Manhattan. They shift credit, on this bank's computers, to the new depositors, but do not affect the Chase Manhattan reserve in the Federal Reserve Bank. Other checks, written upon credit from these loans are deposited in other banks. These checks, whether cleared in a local clearing house or in the Federal Reserve, debit the Chase Manhattan account (reserve) in the Federal Reserve and transfer it as credit to the account (reserve) of the new banks. And in like manner these reserves are shifted from these banks to still other banks and on through the system.

The Sale of Bonds and Notes for Existing Money

Let us now go back to the open market sale of February 2, 1976, and examine the sale of the other securities.

The auction of some $7 billion government bonds did not call for the creation of new money.

The buyers bid on the securities and paid for them with checks drawn on various commercial banks.

The Treasury deposited these checks in various commercial banks. As the checks were cleared in the Federal Reserve Check clearing departments, they shifted reserves from bank to bank.

The following is quoted from *The Federal Reserve Act:*

''All national banking associations designated for that purpose by the Secretary of the Treasury, shall be depositories of public money, under such regulations as may be prescribed by the Secretary of the Treasury; and they may also be employed as financial agents of the government. . . . The Secretary of the Treasury shall distribute the deposits herein provided for, as far as practicable between the different states and sections.'' The Federal Reserve Act — Laws, p. 83, Sec. 5153. Taxes, too, and other revenue may remain in these banks — until called for by the Treasury.

The Reserve

Thus, as we have seen, ''Reserve,'' upon which commercial banks base their loans, has neither substance nor intrinsic value. It is an abstract idea devised to control the amounts of bank-credit commercial banks may create and lend; the amount of money in circulation.

This reserve is nothing more or less than the entry of credit upon the Federal Reserve's ledgers and computers. Its physical existence is nothing more than magnetized particles (bits and bites), on computer discs. This reserve is given to the commercial banks absolutely free.

The Reserve of the Commercial Bank

The reserve of a commercial bank is subject to constant change. A check written on a depositor's account in a commercial bank, deposited in a second commercial bank, and cleared in that region's Federal Reserve Bank, debits the account of the first bank by the amount of the check and shifts that amount of its reserve to the second bank. Thus, in the Federal Reserve there is a constant shift of reserves from the account of one bank to that of others.

The amount of reserve a commercial bank has upon the computers of the Federal Reserve bank, not at any particular time, but on a daily average basis over a stated time, is the base upon which the commercial bank calculates the loans it may make.

56

Just how this reserve is used by the commercial bank will be explained presently after an account of other reserves.

Additional Reserve:
the Federal Reserve Notes

The Federal Reserve notes — the kind we carry in our billfold — are the only United States paper "money" now issued. They are issued in values from $1 to $100. A 1969 Federal Reserve $5 note is illustrated in the lower half of our frontispiece. Its distinctive features are the words "Federal Reserve Note" in the small upper space, and, to the left is the Federal Reserve seal. Each note also bears the distinguishing letter and number of that particular Federal Reserve bank that issued it. These notes are "fiat" money — that is, "they are not convertible into coin or specie of equal value."

The U.S. Comptroller of Currency has the dies made and furnishes the paper; the Treasury Department prints the notes — all paid by the Federal Reserve. The Federal Reserve bank applying for these notes sends, with the request, U.S. Bonds equal to the amount of notes requested. Commercial banks obtain these notes by making application and sending in their promisory note, accompanied by U.S. Bonds of equal value. The bank pays a small rent for the notes. The notes are obligations of the United States. They show the amount the Federal government owes their bearer. The notes are made full legal tender for all debts, public and private.

Act, p. 32, Sec. 16, 2

The government pays these notes by accepting them for taxes.

The production and distribution of coins (now of no intrinsic value) are similar to that of the notes. Both Federal Reserve notes and U.S. coins in a commercial bank are additional reserve. *Act,* p. 39, Sec. 19, 3.

Reserves Through Loans

Though reluctant to do so, the Federal Reserve will, in an emergency, lend reserves to member commercial banks on their promisory notes, secured with government obligations. These loans are of short duration, usually 15 days. At one-half percent higher interest the time may be extended four months. The interest rates for these loans are formally set every 14 days. If the Federal Reserve favors a general expansion of credit, the rate is set lower; if contracture of credit is desired, the rate is set higher.

As these loans must be repaid promptly, the small banks usually go to larger banks to borrow reserve — at interest.

Other Provisions

There are other provisions for rare use in the granting of reserves. In fact, the rules may be suspended altogether.

''The Board of Governors shall be authorized and empowered'' . . . to suspend for a period of not over 30 days and, from time to time, renew such suspension for periods not exceeding 15 days, any reserve requirement in this Act.

(Federal Reserve Act, and amendments through 1971, p. 2.)

The Federal Reserve Methods of Expanding and Contracting the Money in Circulation

When expansion of the economy is desired, the usual method of achieving this is as follows:

The New York Regional Bank is instructed to create the desired amount of new money. In this case, let us say $5 billion. It does this by making a record of the transaction and entering that number of dollars of "reserve" on its computer. The Federal Reserve then buys, through the open market, $5 billion in government bonds, paying for them with checks drawn on the newly created money. The bonds are put in the vault of the Federal Reserve Bank. The sellers of the bonds deposit the checks in commercial banks.

These commercial banks send the checks to the Federal Reserve for payment. In the check clearing department of the Federal Reserve, the checks are paid by deducting that amount, $5 billion (just created), from the account of the Federal Reserve and crediting it to the commercial banks.

The canceled checks, stamped "paid," are returned to the commercial banks and from there to their writers. The $5 billion now stands, on the Federal Reserve computers, to the credit of those commercial banks, and is added "reserve" against which these banks may and do lend.

As checks from these loans pass between commercial banks and are cleared in the Federal Reserve bank, the reserves are broken up and shifted back and forth upon the Federal Reserve computers. Some of the checks, and thus some of credit for reserves, trickles down to small commercial banks, enabling them also to increase their loans.

To contract (lessen) the amount of money in circulation, the reverse of the above method is used, that is, the Federal Reserve banks, through the open market, sells U.S. Bonds from their vaults.

The buyers' checks, drawn upon funds in commercial banks, are made out to the Federal Reserve, are received at the Federal Reserve's check clearing department. The checks are stamped "paid" and are returned to the commercial bank and on to the writer. The Federal Reserve debits the account (reserve) of the commercial banks to that amount. The money, nothing but electrical particles in a computer, is extinguished. This cancelation of reserve, lessening the commercial bank's ability to lend, forces a chain reaction, lessening loans and thus reducing money in circulation.

Other Duties

I. THE CLEARANCE OF CHECKS

An extremely important and highly efficient service rendered by the Federal Reserve is the clearance of checks. Local checks are cleared by local clearing houses and the net balance of each bank sent to the Federal Reserve. Intra-district checks are cleared through the Federal Reserve.

In 1972, it was estimated that some 8 billion checks transferring about $3 trillion, were cleared in a year. When electric circuits connecting all banks are completed, the clearance of checks will be almost instantaneous.

II. REGULATION OF CREDIT ON STOCK EXCHANGE

"For the purpose of preventing excessive use of credit . . . the Board of Governors shall . . . prescribe rules and regulations with respect to the amount of credit that may be initially extended and subsequently maintained on any security." Government involved securities are excepted. *Act,* p. 137.

(It follows that the great financiers who have access to this information and have, also, control of vast amounts of money, have an enormous advantage.)

III. STATISTICS AND FINANCIAL REPORTS

The gathering of statistics relating to the economic condition of the nation, and their periodic report, is of great importance.

IV. CONTROL OF MEMBER BANKS

The Federal Reserve exerts a watchful control over the management and fiscal condition of its member banks. Its own examiners, sometimes along with state examiners, examine the System's state member banks. The Federal Reserve usually, but not always, accepts the reports of the examiners of Comptroller of Currency for the good condition of the national banks. Along with any Federal Reserve criticism are suggestions for correction.

Income and Disbursements of the Federal Reserve Proper

For the year 1968, over 95 percent of its income was derived from government securities obtained as we have seen — an expense to the taxpayer.

A statement of disbursements is published in a pamphlet, *U.S. Currency,* published by the Federal Reserve Board, 1969. It states:

"All earnings are paid into the United States Treasury after payment of expenses, the statutory six percent dividend to member banks, and any additions to surplus necessary to maintain each Reserve bank's surplus at an amount equal to its paid-in capital stock. In 1968, these additions to surplus amount to $30 million . . . in event of their liquidation, any

61

surplus of the Reserve banks, after meeting all obligations, would become the property of the United States Government.''

The exact amount of the surplus, December 31, 1968, was $628,768,650. Note this statement carefully. It was enough to buy the Federal Reserve for the people without an additional dollar outlay. The capital stock varies slightly as members come and go. On December 31, 1970, it was $702 million and the surplus was the same. In 1978 this figure was $1.078 billion.

Mr. Patman states that the officials of the Federal Reserve use the bank's funds as if they were personal funds. He names gifts, scholarships to the families of personnel, yachting parties, and the like.

We notice that not counting salaries and fees of some $130 million, there are retirement and other benefits costing that year some $20.92 million and expenses for the Board of Governors of over $14 million.

The Federal Reserve banks claim to be quasi-public and as such have many important privileges. *There is no auditing of their books by any regulatory agency, no operating tax, no income tax.*

In reality, the Federal Reserve System is a private banker's bank, controlled by international financiers, totally independent of our government, and in its many aspects and connections, largely run for private profit.

How the Federal Reserve Gives United States Bonds to Private Banks

When the Federal Reserve, through its manipulations, has amassed, absolutely free, quite a pile of government bonds, it gives them to the commercial banks, chiefly to the great banks.

Mr. Patman devotes a chapter to this: "How the Federal Reserve Gives Away Public Funds to Private Banks." He gives two examples.

In the early part of 1958, the Federal Reserve, by lowering the Reserve requirements, allowed private commercial banks to increase their bank credit money supply by approximately $10 billion. The stated reason was to strengthen the banks and make it possible for them to make more loans to business (there was a recession at that time). Instead of lending out this $10 billion, the private banks used this bank-credit money (nothing but entries in ledgers and the filling out of blank checks) to acquire an additional $10 billion of interest-bearing government bonds — a profit to the bankers, a taxation on the people.

Did the banks need the money? No. Although there was a recession, the bankers' earnings were up. Furthermore, most of the $10 billion was given to a very few large banks which had enjoyed extremely high incomes. Two percent of the banks received three-fourths of the bonds. *(A Primer on Money,* pages 91-92.) This type of bond purchase must go on all the time.

In 1959, the Federal Reserve gave outright, free, to the commercial banks $16.8 billion of government securities. How many billions in government bonds the Federal Reserve has passed into private banks and then on into private hands would be hard to estimate. In 1976, Mr. Patman stated, "$93 billion paid-up government bonds are held by the Federal Reserve."

Though the commercial member banks still claim the Federal Reserve stock and still receive annually six percent interest upon it, they have long ago drawn out all their money. In the *Primer,* p. 37, Mr. Patman tells how the bankers play upon the general public's ignorance and misunderstanding in their raids on the public treasury.

The truth is, he says, "The private banks, collectively, have deposited not a penny of their own, or their depositors' funds with the Federal Reserve banks."

On page 39 *(The Primer)* Mr. Patman, speaking as of 1959, says: "Let us assume — for the sake of analysis, that the $1.5 billion of reserve which the banks of the system had to their credit in 1917 came about through actual deposits of cash by the banks. We may say, then, that in return for this $1.5 billion in cash, the banks have been paid back in cash $28 billion. They still have left another $18.5 billion in reserve accounts, a circumstance which entitles them to have outstanding seven times the amount of government securities and other interest paying securities and loans" (through Fractional Reserve Banking).

Ownership

Differing opinions abound as to who owns the Federal Reserve.

Jim Townsend, editor of *The National Educator* and chairman of the R.O.C. movement (Redeem Our Country by abolishing the Fed), gave front-page space to this issue in January of 1983.

"The hoax Federal Reserve bankers and their employees, congressmen in both Houses, have sold to the public for the past 69 years, has finally been exposed by the Ninth Circuit Court in a decision of 'Lewis vs. United States.' The court found the Federal Reserve banks were separate corporations owned by commercial banks in its region. In plain English, Federal Reserve banks are privately owned, and the fact the Federal Reserve Board regulates the Reserve banks does not make them federal agencies under the Act."

Regardless of this recent court decision, however, powerful historical evidence exists to the contrary. Wright Patman's

Primer on Money records the following statements:

"In a letter to Representative Wright Patman, dated April 18, 1941, Marriner S. Eccles, Chairman of the Board of (Fed) Governors, stated: 'This so-called stock ownership, however, is more in the nature of an enforced subscription to the capital of the Federal Reserve banks than an ownership in the usual sense' " (page 77).

And again, William McChesney Martin, then chairman of the board, said in 1956, "The banks do not own the Federal Reserve System" (page 78).

Congressman Wright Patman continues:

"Hearings before various congressional committees have established clearly that this stock is not stock in the ordinary meaning of the term.

"(1) It carries no proprietary interest. In this respect, the stock is unlike the stock of any private corporation.

"(2) It cannot be sold or pledged for loans. It thus does not represent an ownership claim.

"(3) In the event of the dissolution of the Federal Reserve banks, the net assets after payment of the liabilities and repayment of the stock go to the U.S. Treasury rather than the private banks.

"(4) The stock does not carry the ordinary voting rights of stock. The method of electing officers of the Federal Reserve banks is in no way connected to the amount of stock ownership. Instead, each bank in a district has one vote within its class, regardless of its stock-ownership" (page 81).

As originally stated, the Federal Reserve Act was created to discount eligible bank paper. The joining banks put in three percent of their capital to create a fund to lend to banks on this good paper. This discounting of paper has not been done in years, and the bankers' money lies in the Federal Reserve vaults.

The United States Treasury, through taxation and borrowing, pays high interest on government bonds scattered throughout the world, and also on the U.S. bonds still in the Federal Reserve vaults. It pays this interest to the Federal Reserve. From such interest (on bonds in its vault), the Federal Reserve pays a statutory six percent interest on the commercial bankers' idle funds in the Federal Reserve vaults. The Federal Reserve's physical plant and its operating expenses are also paid for from this U.S. Treasury payment. The remainder of the Treasury payment should be returned to the U.S. Treasury, according to law.

The word "stock," as used here, is like all the other words and dealings of these bankers — a ploy and attempt to confuse.

Lending Institutions

Banks, the kind you deal with, have always been greatly favored by law, and have been exempt from many taxes. The theory was that they would build up the community in which they operated. At first, bank directors were required to live in the district where their banks were located. Today many banks are ruled by absentee directors — their owners unknown — the titles held in the names of nominees.

In the United States, as of January 1, 1977, there were 14,145 lending institutions recognized as banks by the Federal bank supervisory agencies. All operate on money which in the past, has been created and issued by the Federal Reserve, but almost two-thirds of these banks were then not members of the Federal Reserve. They operated under charters of various states. The rules and regulations of some states must have been lax indeed. Read the following:

Federal Reserve Member Banks

On the above date the Federal Reserve membership consisted of 4,735 national banks (membership required) and

1,023 state commercial banks (membership optional).

There was then a decline in state bank membership. The Chairman of Citicorp complained that in 1977, his bank lost $80 million by being a member of the Federal Reserve.

As of mid-1978, member banks controlled 72.5 percent of United States bank deposits — down from 86 percent in 1965.

In the following explanations, the term "commercial bank" refers to member banks — under direct control of the Federal Reserve.

We have seen how the Federal Reserve provides reserves for its member banks, and how it keeps track of these reserves. We shall now see how these banks use these "reserves" in making loans.

Today's Fractional Reserve System

Two factors determine the amount of bank credit a commercial bank may, at any given moment, create and lend at interest.

1. The Amount of the Bank's Reserve,

    a) On the Federal Reserve computers (a new deposit, or unused old deposits).

    b) The amount of Federal Reserve notes and coins in its vault.

2. The Reserve Requirement:

    The Federal Reserve sets this ratio. If expansion of credit is desired the percentage of reserve required is low — if contraction is desired, it is raised.

THE FRACTIONAL RESERVE FORMULA
A × B = C

Let "A" stand for any unused reserve a commercial bank may have at any given time.

Let "B" stand for the allowable expansion of this reserve. (In checking accounts, this coefficient or factor is usually 6 or 8 — it has been much higher. In savings or time deposits, it is usually 30.

It follows that "C" represents the amount of bank credit which may be created and loaned, at interest from any given deposit.

These facts are simply stated in the following copies of letters from the Congressional Research Service of the Library of Congress and Congressman James A. Haley.[5]

Concrete Examples

Demand Deposits

Suppose a customer comes into a commercial bank and deposited a check for $1,000 in his checking account. He could, on demand, draw this out at any time. Such a deposit is called a "demand deposit."

This creates, in the Federal Reserve, for the bank, a reserve of $1,000.

The Federal Reserve requirements for demand deposits expansion vary, but suppose that at the time of this deposit the factor "B" is 7. Thus we have, in accordance with our formula:

$$\$1,000 \times 7 = \$7,000$$

Thus the commercial bank, from this $1,000 deposit, may create and lend $7,000 at interest.

THE LIBRARY OF CONGRESS

Congressional Research Service

WASHINGTON, D.C. 20540

November 29, 1971

To: The Honorable John Rarick

From: Economics Division

Subject: Information on Federal Reserve Lending Policies and the
          Multiplier Effect of Adjustment in Member Bank
          Reserve Requirements

The enclosed pamphlet explains the impact on individual member banks of Federal Reserve creation of credit through adjusments of the reserve requirements (see markers).

Your constituent is most probably referring--speaking of a 1-32 ratio-- of the coefficient of bank expansion. This term represents the ratio of total potential expansion of the amount of excess legal reserves. This coefficient is generally considered to be in the 1-6 or 1-8 range for demand deposits in member banks and generally in a 1-30 range for savings and other time deposits in these banks. This coefficient means that a one dollar deposit in a member commercial bank, in excess of legal reserve requirements, will usually result in a credit expansion of six to eight dollars if it is a demand deposit and thirty dollars if it is a savings or other time deposit.

Michael J. McCarthy
Economic Analyst

JAMES A. HALEY
7TH DIST., FLORIDA

WASHINGTON ADDRESS:
ROOM 1236 LONGWORTH BUILDING

HOME ADDRESS:
P.O. BOX 1053
SARASOTA, FLORIDA

COMMITTEES:
INTERIOR AND INSULAR AFFAIRS
CHAIRMAN, SUBCOMMITTEE ON
INDIAN AFFAIRS
MEMBER, SUBCOMMITTEE ON
IRRIGATION AND RECLAMATION
MEMBER, SUBCOMMITTEE ON
TERRITORIES AND INSULAR AFFAIRS
MEMBER, SUBCOMMITTEE ON
THE ENVIRONMENT
VETERANS' AFFAIRS
MEMBER, SUBCOMMITTEE ON
HOSPITALS
JOINT COMMITTEE ON
NAVAJO-HOPI INDIAN
ADMINISTRATION

WASHINGTON STAFF:
MISS ALICE MYERS
PALMETTO, FLORIDA

MRS. MARILEE B. MacNICHOL
RIVERVIEW, FLORIDA

DISTRICT OFFICES:
BARTOW, FLORIDA
R. ELMO HOOD

FORT MYERS, FLORIDA
MRS. BURNETT BLOODWORTH

Congress of the United States
House of Representatives
Washington, D.C. 20515
November 17, 1971

Mr. Mark Andrews
Box 9
Cape Coral, Florida 33904

Dear Mr. Andrews.

This is to acknowledge your last three letters dated November 9, 11, and 14, 1971 concerning the Federal Reserve and the United Nations.

You have asked whether the FED banks can loan $32 for every $1 they have in Reserves, whether member banks can loan $10 for every $1 they have in Reserves, and what law permits this. As a spokesman for the FED explained, although it is an oversimplification of the problem, the answers to your first two questions are yes. Since you asked that I not send any more research materials to you, I will simply refer you to section 19 of the Federal Reserve Act of 1913 for the law you were looking for. You probably have that document since I sent you a copy of it on June 23, 1970. As to my opinion of the FED system, I think it is the best one devised so far and I have yet to see a more workable alternative.

In response to your question as to how I stand on Rep. Rarick's bill to buy back the FED, I will call your attention to my comments on this subject in several of the many letters I have written to you in the past. In my September 11, 1970 letter I stated, "Insofar as Congressman Rarick's and Congressman Patman's proposals are concerned, I will make this statement: Congressman Patman has had this kind of proposal before the Congress for many years and he cannot get this legislation out of the committee which he chairs. It is my observation that the only alternative is to move in the way suggested by the Board of Governors (of the FED)." I said in the same letter concerning the fact that there is no need to buy back the FED, "There would be no need to do anything other than to repeal the Act and all the assets would then revert to the Government after the member banks had paid off their obligations."

Sincerely yours,

James A. Haley
Congressman, 7th District

Time Deposits

Now suppose that this customer had deposited the check for $1,000 not in a checking account but in a savings or other time account. In this case, he cannot, without penalty, withdraw this money until the expiration date on his saving certificate. This type of deposit is called a time deposit. As we have seen, the factor "B" in time deposits is usually 30. It follows that:

$$\$1,000 \times 30 = \$30,000$$

That is, the commercial bank can create $30,000 out of the thin air and lend it at interest.

If there were only one commercial bank and all of its checks came back to it, it could, like a goldsmith, safely place an entire deposit in reserve and at once create and lend, at interest, the full potential bank credit.

There are, however, many banks, and the manager of a bank receiving a deposit knows that some checks which will be written by the depositor and the borrower, will be sent to other banks and that these will carry with them a shift of reserves. He, therefore, places the deposit in reserve, and on a portion of this, creates and lends that amount of bank-credit he deems safe. The rest of the deposit is kept in reserve to satisfy the checks deposited in other banks.

On the transaction we are following, the next bank, or banks, to receive some of these checks, also uses the safe percentage in creating and lending bank credit. This continues until all of the original deposit has gone into reserve and there has been created and loaned, at interest, from 6 to 30 times the amount of the deposit.

At the same time, all banks are engaged in continuing such chains, and checks (deposits usually) by the thousands pass from bank to bank.

As borrowers pay their notes, the principal of each note is extinguished — the reserve remains as basis for new loans unless checked out.

The yearly optimum potential gross profit from the transactions described above varies from well over half the amount of the original deposits, to over five times that amount.

Thus, the amount of interest on loans created from bank credit divided up within the banking system is a geometric progression. This interest is retained by the banks as part of their gross profits.

A Borrower

Suppose a man comes into a large bank and wishes to borrow a million dollars to build a motel. The bank may not have the money, nor need have it. In normal times, and if within its reserve requirements, the bank's official could take a million dollar mortgage on the future motel and create the money. All he would have to do would be to order a clerk to write the man's name in a ledger, put it in with a typewriter, or enter it in a computer, and after the name state a credit of the figure $1,000,000. The borrower is then given a deposit slip showing this amount, and a book of blank checks. This money did not exist a minute before. There it is now — created by an entry on a computer — as good as any other money!

It is said that money is the only "tangible" thing man has ever created; that all else he has made by changing the form of existing things; but here he creates something which has an exact value — out of nothing.

The explanation is that modern money is not a material thing. It is simply a permit — issued by the bankers — to carry out a transaction. The evidence of this permit is created from existing things — from paper and ink, and from an electrical current and particles on computer discs.

The interest charged on these permits (loans) is collected from labor. It is, to the banker, "in the clear." That is, it is not controlled by the Federal Reserve. After expenses, bankers use this interest as claims for property — real wealth.

Commercial Bank Profits

Bank profits have never been small. In the early twenties Congressman Charles A. Lindbergh, Sr., wrote:

"From testimony given by George F. Baker, President of First National Bank of New York City, before the Committee appointed to investigate the money trust, we learn that the operation of a single bank produced in fifty years, profits equal to $86 million or 172 times its original capital."

With refined methods of the fifty years since then, it takes little imagination to believe that the bankers, dealing in billions of dollars, at high interest rates, have made fantastic profits.

There are those who point out that some banks pay small dividends on their stock. Large salaries and expense accounts to their real owners, and the fact that banks are wont to expand and to pay stock dividends instead of cash dividends account for this.

For the first great New York bank we looked up, there was a 1969 dividend of only 4 percent. There was, however, in May of that year a 50 percent stock dividend. The bank, of course, expects a return on this "new capital." And then, as we shall see, banks use much, if not most of their earnings, to buy stocks and other real wealth.

Along with the high interest rates, 10 percent in October 1969, and 20 percent in the spring of 1980, there are other angles to lending.

The Charlotte Observer, October 11, 1969, stated that money lending institutions are revising the old practice of demanding, in addition, a "kicker" — a percentage of the price, or else of the gross income from the project financed. At times, there is a demand for part of the "action." This is the way the Mellon family, in the 1890's, got in on the ground floor of the aluminum industry. Sometimes the lending institution demands that it be given an option to buy the project when the mortgage is finally paid — at the then tax-depreciated book value; or again it may demand a part of the title.

Each year the Federal Reserve pays commercial banks six percent interest on some $900 million of Federal Reserve Stock. On stock issued before March 1943, this interest is tax-free.

Forty years ago, a branch bank at my hometown occupied the ground floor of a narrow store building. Today, its great, massive, beautifully appointed building occupies half a city block. It has 21 secondary branch banks scattered through its neighborhood. In the past few years the stock of this bank has split and split again — 1978 earnings were 25.7 percent above 1977.

The Insiders

Those who control large banks receive large salaries and dividends on their stock. This, however, is not the whole story. Senate investigations afford some insight into methods used and advantages enjoyed by those who control banks.

Some make large favorable loans to members of their family or to friends.

Through so-called "correspondent accounts" owners of banks make deposits in other banks, and borrow ten times as much. In one such deal investigated, a banker deposited $250,000 in a great northern bank and, on this, borrowed $2,600,000.

Could the basis for this have been a mere $10,000 deposit

74

in the first bank? We know that a time deposit may be blown up 30 times. And taking this blown-up deposit, did the great northern bank blow it up again into $4,900,000, not only furnishing this loan, but creating an additional $2,300,000 which they could lend at interest? I do not know, nor do I know what other favored treatment was given to this little banker. Another bank which provided such funds charged little or no interest for its officials, saying, ''He did not pay for the trouble,'' presumably clerical expenses.

It is reported that 93 percent of the nation's banks engage in correspondent accounts.

A Lesson in Progression

Like giant trees of the forest that grew from tiny seeds, the great banks and their conglomerates had an almost insignificant beginning.

The trunks of the little trees slowly reached the size of a pencil. Each year each cell in their tiny annual, outer, ring divided into two, and these into four or more, and added a new ring. As ring upon ring was added, each greater in circumference than the one before, the number of cells added each year progressively increased. Growth became more and more rapid. The trees became the giants we see today. Their growth is, however, wisely limited by nature. Only cells of the last ring divide, and the trees grow old and die.

The banks, small in the beginning, manufactured money, multiplied it, loaned it at interest, and doubled it. More money was produced, added to this, and all loaned. This manipulation has been repeated, year after year, and is continuing — not only with currently produced money but with the first, the middle and the last, all doubling, and doubling, and doubling again. Here there is no limit; expansion is now almost explosive.

Let us look at the mathematics underlying the awesome power residing in the privilege of issuing money and lending it at interest.

The Infinite Claims of Interest

Long custom requires that we accept the burden of interest as if it were a law of nature. But interest was devised by man, and as it is levied, is ruinous. It grows, like an inverted pyramid, toward infinity. It is important that the reader understand this last statement. One simple example tells the tale (calculated in 1974).

Had one cent been loaned at six percent compound interest at the beginning of the Christian era, the amount of money due may be determined with simple arithmetic.

There have been 1974 years since the birth of Christ.

Any amount of money (in this case, one cent), loaned at six percent compound interest doubles at approximately 11.89 yearly intervals. Therefore, divide 1974 by 11.89. This gives 166 — the number of times the principle (one cent) must be doubled.

First $\$.01 \times 2 = \$.02$ at end of first period

then $\$.02 \times 2 = \$.04$ at end of second period

$\$.04 \times 2 = \$.08$ at end of third period.

and so on, doubling 166 times.

The equation was solved in this way, and also by an expert mathematician on a computer for the year 1974. The mind cannot grasp the fantastic amount of money called for by this claim. To assist a little, these dollars were converted into gold at the price of $35 an ounce.

After consulting reference books and doing a little simple arithmetic, it was found that if every heavenly body in the solar system — the mighty sun (a million times larger than the earth) and all its planets Mercury, Venus, the World, Mars, Jupiter, Saturn, Uranus, Neptune and Pluto, together with their satellites were made of pure gold, they would not — by weight — pay for the use of that one copper penny — no, not nearly. It is now 1983. But for the inflated price of gold it would take two solar systems to settle the claim.

Suppose that penny had been loaned at 20 percent compound interest — the prime interest of today — and doubling the principal in less than every four years had, by now, 1983 years since the birth of Christ, doubled it some 500 times.

To satisfy the claim would, perhaps, take in gold the weight of most of the stars in the milky way.

The disastrous effects (envisioned) of such loans over such a long period of time is now being brought on in a comparative short time by the magnitude of modern loans.

The great financiers, usurping the right to create money, manipulate and lend not pennies but bank-credit running into hundreds of billions of dollars — at higher and higher interest.

Money is loaned in fixed, finite amounts. Interest claims are infinite and are not provided for. The chance of borrowers as a whole, to return the principal and to get the money for interest, is simply nonexistent. Interest must be paid by the surrender of property.

There is no limit or end to this drain upon society. Banks and their corporations are, by law, endowed with endless life.

A Summary

We have seen that at the very first days of this nation the bankers gained the privilege of printing paper money and lending it at interest; that later they suppressed Lincoln's United States Note; and then, under the pretense of reform, secured the Federal Reserve Act of 1913. This act, with its subsequent amendments, has done away with all "United States" money, and has placed the nation's monetary and financial system under the absolute control of bankers. They operate the system as their own private business, primarily for their own private profit.

The United States Government is not allowed to issue its own simple, interest-free notes and use these as money. It must, however, guarantee the notes issued by Federal Reserve banks which are used as money. The government must also issue and exchange interest bearing United States bonds for all these notes it is forced to borrow. Once issued, these bonds or their replacements are held as a permanent debt.

The Federal Reserve system is based upon a large and ever-growing government debt and nothing else. This debt has now reached enormous proportions.

Much of these U.S. Bonds are now the property of the financiers who handled them. The nation's yearly $120 billion dollar deficit is for these men — soaked up as by a sponge. Financiers collect interest on these bonds, paid for by taxation.

The following is a schematic diagram of this present monetary system. It also shows the basket of those who devised it.

PRESENT MONETARY SYSTEM
AND THE
FINANCIERS

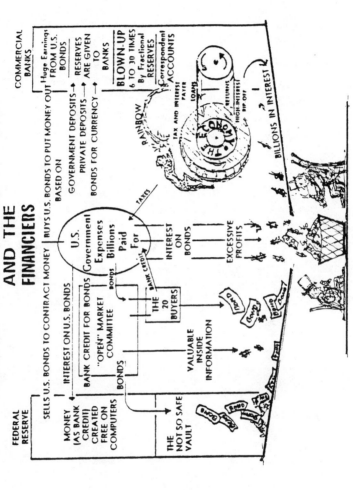

CHAPTER 7

Bankers as Public Officials

It is usual to appoint a banker as Secretary of the Treasury. Most, perhaps all of those appointed have lobbied against the public interest; have joined in lawsuits to force through denied mergers or to throw off legal restraints. We cannot expect such men to wholeheartedly serve the people against their own kind. The conflict of interest is inherent and is dangerous.

Secretary Henry Fowler suppressed the United States Note in the last days of October 1968. A few days later, November 8th, 1968, he resigned, effective December 20, 1968.

On December 3, 1968, it was reported that "Secretary of the Treasury Henry Fowler announced today that he plans to become a partner of the New York Investment Banking Firm of Goldman, Sachs and Company on January 1st." (This is one of the world's largest banks.)

Such shunting of bankers into the government and back to the banks is usual.

In early September 1978, Arthur Burns, age 74, financial advisor to presidents and recent chairman of the Federal

Reserve, and of course, drawing its pensions, was employed at a large retainer by Lazard Freres, one of the nation's most progressive investment banking firms.

Federal Reserve Chairman Miller was not only president of the giant Textron Corporation; he was also a bank director, and for a number of years its representative with the Federal Reserve.

Within a month after assuming his position as head of the Federal Reserve, Mr. Miller decreed that commercial member banks could draw money from depositors' saving accounts to cover check overdrafts, thus making saving accounts upon which a small interest is paid, virtual checking accounts. This interest will entice many depositors to put most of their money in savings accounts. On a deeper look, this innovation will permit commercial banks to further expand their loans, for with this money, they can use the one to 30 fractional reserve formula instead of the lower checking account formula.

Mr. Miller attempted to take the money which taxpayers yearly pay in as interest on the U.S. Bonds in Federal Reserve vaults, and divide it up among member commercial banks.

Stopped in a confrontation with Congressmen, he sent to Congress a bill proposing to pay these commercial banks two percent interest on this mythical reserve. This interest may sound low. It is probably calculated to take all this money.

Remembrance of the newscast, in which Federal Reserve Chairman G.W. Miller so indignantly and so arrogantly reminded Congressmen of his authority, is brought vividly to mind by a short article in *The Miami Herald,* March 3, 1979. Evidently Mr. Miller used that authority and changed Federal Reserve rules — to give commercial banks more profit. The article states that in the face of opposition by major banking organizations, Henry Reuss, Chairman of House Banking Committee, backed down and shelved a bill which would have required banks to hold reserves in the Federal Reserve. Banking groups insisted, ". . . on a voluntary reserve system and that interest be paid on reserves."

In mid-1980 we find Mr. Miller promoted to be Secretary of the Treasury; and Mr. Paul A. Volcker, a member of David Rockefeller's Chase Manhattan Bank and of the Trilateral Commission, became Chairman of the Board of Governors of the Federal Reserve.

CHAPTER 8

Financiers Never Rest

Credit Cards

The bankers are issuing their charge cards. These cards are convenient, can best be managed by the commercial banks, and will for them supply a new function and an additional source of revenue. Handled for the common good at a reasonable interest, these cards will be a welcome addition to the monetary system; but is that the purpose?

The customer pays nothing direct if the account is settled within 25 days. After that he is charged 18 percent interest. The price to the retailer varies and may be from two to five percent — not per annum, but upon each transaction. This last charge is, of course, passed on to all customers.

The Charlotte Observer, April 26, 1970, told what a bonanza the credit card is to the banks: ''The credit card business in the United States has increased the price of goods and services by seven percent.''

The bankers' take from this source is fantastic. The bankers may argue that this is justified, due to the merchants' saving in bookkeeping. But are such profits from the control of credit just? Should any organization by the use of a machine, the computer, turn tens of thousands of office workers adrift and claim all possible of their wages, and raise prices on everything the dispossessed must buy?

The Christian Science Monitor, March 18, 1981, stated that Master Charge and Visa together now handle $54 billion in charge loans a year.

There is now a move to deposit payrolls in banks to be debited by computers — the laborer never seeing his money. This is but one outcropping of the ferment stirring within banking circles, as those in control move to extend their power.

Thomas Porter in *The Green Magicians,* takes a dim view of all this as he explains the process. Mr. Porter says that according to George W. Mitchell, the member of the Federal Reserve Board who is in charge of this development, it is planned to establish a checkless, cashless society in the United States.

Money and checks will be replaced by credit cards. These are to be introduced in all states and in all countries. They will be placed under the World Bank. Then when credit cards get lost, duplicated and so forth, a laser marking will be placed on the body.

"When all currency has been withdrawn from circulation," Mr. Porter says, "nothing can be bought or sold without a charge card. Every sale will require a tribute to the banks." Mr. Porter calls attention to a remarkable prophecy from the Bible, ". . . and no man might buy or sell save he that has the mark or the name of the beast or the number of his name" (Revelation 13:17).[1]

Proposed Banking Law

The international banks in New York are now pressing for a law which will allow them to establish branch banks all over the nation. This will enable them to compete with and take over small local banks.

According to *The Spotlight,* February 9, 1981, the Carter Administration, just before leaving office, brought in a report recommending that the McFadden Act of 1934 be phased out, thus allowing a megabank-dominated national banking system.

The report recommends that this system be implemented in stages: that at first only Federal Chartered banks be allowed to go national. "Not surprisingly almost all of the country's largest institutions (i.e., Bank of America, Chase Manhattan, Citibank, First National of Chicago, etc.), hold federal charters under this plan; therefore restrictions on interstate banking would not only be abolished, but they would be abolished in such a way as to allow the super banks a virtually insurmountable head start."[2]

Bank Holding Companies

Bank holding companies allow the banks to compete with their customers in almost all businesses. The method is for those who control the bank policies to form a new corporation — a holding company — by an exchange, with themselves, of all a bank's stock for stock in a new corporation. The holding company becomes the owner of the bank, and the bank, while apparently operating in its traditional fashion is, in fact, the private mint of the holding company. Its main function is then to create a supply of money for its holding company, to finance their purchases, and manipulations, of almost unlimited varieties of businesses.

Office buildings which banks have built have emptied many other buildings. This is bad enough, but read the following list tabulated by Roy Covington in *The Charlotte Observer:* "Placed under the First Union Bancorp 'umbrella' have been these subsidiaries: First National Bank, Cameron Brown Company, the Mortgage Banking Firm, Kincade Advertising Agency, General Finance Agency, First Card Corporation, Cameron Brown Capital Corporation, Charge Plans, Inc., Saint Lewis Corp., and Gotham Corporation (both real estate holding companies), National Investment Co., and House of Rothschilds, Inc., a creator of check design company." Other areas mentioned include acting as stock brokers, "data processing services, mutual funds, leasing, insurance companies and travel checks."[3]

These holding companies have made great strides in the years since Mr. Covington compiled his modest list. No enterprise is too great for them; none too small. They build cities; they vend ice cream on the streets.

A private businessman attempting to enter or remain in business must buy from those he is ordered to deal with; his attorney is selected for him at a named fee; he must insure with the bank's insurance company; and, if the bank will lend to him, he must borrow at high interest from the bank owning the company with which he is competing.

Under the caption "Bank Holding Firms Getting Some Big Breaks Tax-wise," in *The Charlotte Observer,* May 1, 1975, Clark Hoyt says that taking advantage of special provisions written into federal tax laws, several of the nation's largest bank holding companies, *while paying no federal tax,* were eligible for substantial refunds! "With combined profits of $332.5 million in 1974, Chase Manhattan and Chemical of New York were eligible to collect $21.6 million from the U.S. Treasury."

The earnings (levies on society) of many bank holding

companies roll up yearly — like giant snowballs. For the last quarter of 1978, the Chase Manhattan Corporation reports a 62 percent increase over the same quarter of 1977. Its 1979 profit was 58 percent higher than its 1978 profit.

In every city one may see new bank buildings trimmed in gleaming chrome, plate glass and marble, rising high and clean above the squalor of those they have despoiled. These buildings stand like fortresses, as if guarding great wealth. They don't. If their thick walls were torn away, we would find that the banker's stock in trade is little more than notations of names and numbers, and magnetized particles they have entered upon their computers.

Sketch of Charlotte, North Carolina, skyline
and its six bank buildings.

Attempt to Curb Holding Companies

Congressman Wright Patman, then Chairman of the House Banking and Currency Committee, attempted to curb the bank holding companies. Let us review a few reports that came from Capital Hill while this important piece of legislation was being considered — legislation that would mean billions of dollars to the bankers.

In 1968, the records of the Federal Reserve listing of the

top 20 stockholders of the national banks contained the names of dozens of congressmen and their relatives. On Capital Hill, bank interest has become a preoccupation of many legislators. It was known that 12 members of the House Banking and Currency Committee and 94 members of the full House body had interest in banks, savings and loan institutions, or bank holding companies.

In *The Christian Science Monitor,* August 5, 1959, Mr. Patman charged that banks raise an annual kitty of millions of dollars to pay lobbyists and to be doled out to congressmen. In his address before the National Press Club, July 31, 1969, Mr. Patman said this lobby ''has offered large amounts of bank stock and bank directorships to committee members, immediate loan service to freshmen congressmen on their arrival in Washington, campaign contributions, and mass mailing to stockholders in behalf of certain political candidates.''

Mr. Patman's crusade against bank holding companies came quietly to an end December 27, 1970. The bill, as passed, confirmed holding companies formed before June 30, 1968. It also provided that decisions as to future applications to form holding companies be left to the discretion of Federal Reserve officials; in reality the great financiers — the very ones the bill was supposed to control.

Foreign Exchange

Great international banks have departments that trade in foreign monies. These buy any foreign money called for; and as ''Bills of Exchange,'' at an advanced price, sell the money to importers who use it to pay for foreign goods. The unit ratio of the value of any two monies is the ''Rate of Exchange'' of the two monies. Normally, this rate tends to be stable. There are, however, factors that weaken the value of a nation's money and then speculators, thirsting for profit, attack it.

The International Monetary Fund, 1944, and other organizations, were formed in an attempt to stabilize the Rate of Exchange.

The American dollar was selected as the basis. It was said to be "as good as gold." Although there was no law requiring this, the notes were exchangeable (to foreigners) for gold on demand. The troops were left in Europe. There was a giveaway to foreign countries. The Vietnam War drew many billions away. U.S. financiers carried out vast amounts of U.S. dollars. In 1968, it became apparent that we had only a token of gold as compared to the vast amount of our existing money. Speculators, seeing that conversion of our money was impossible, drove against our money, demanding gold for their Federal Reserve Notes. They hoped to force an official increase in the price of gold. This would allow them to exchange it for Federal Reserve Notes at a profit.

On August 15, 1971, President Nixon put a stop to the conversion of our paper money into gold.

The Gold Standard

Of course, gold is desirable. It glitters, is imperishable, and is a rarity. It is not, however, as useful as steel and plastic and glass of which our cars and appliances are made, nor as desirable as shelter and clothes, or food when one is hungry. Its high price came about because its connection with money. First used in three-barter, gold was finally coined. It was used as money for 2600 years, first as a 100 percent gold reserve, and then as a fractional reserve. The use of gold as money was still a type of three-barter. As a third commodity in trade, gold could be hoarded, its use denied to many.

In all those years, there must have been countless millions of abuses — well known are two large ones in our own country. In 1749 the King of England ordered the colonies to return to specie payment. Most people could not get gold to pay their taxes and saw their property sold to insiders, who knew the blow was coming, for a tenth of its value. And again on "Black Friday," September 24, 1869, Jay Gould and John Fisk, Jr., cornered the nation's gold, causing a severe monetary panic.

History also tells us of many shady manipulations of gold as money. In the Cleveland administration financiers brought large amounts of paper money to the Treasury and demanded that it be redeemed with gold. They would then require that the Treasury replenish its gold reserve by buying the gold back — at a profit to them. This was done by changing tags on the same gold in the Treasury.

Our monetary system has always been inherently evil, controlled by bankers who made it their business to take from it all possible private gain — by fair means or foul. The nation suffered depression after depression. The fractional gold standard was but a manipulated part of the whole. It was discontinued in 1933. This act was simply another step in the plundering of this nation.

In going off the gold standard there was no honest reason why the people's gold was taken from them. The financiers who inspired the taking wanted the gold. They took not only gold coins, but gold certificates and gold bullion. They evidently expected to put us back on the gold standard with great profit to themselves.

(In discontinuing silver money, the Treasury set the date: June 24, 1968, after which it would exchange no more silver coins for silver certificates. The Treasury let the people keep their silver coins. The silver certificates became ordinary circulating notes. That was the honest way to have gone off the gold standard.)

After the gold was placed in Fort Knox, foreigners could draw it out for American paper money, but the American people could not. That is, none except the bankers. They could find a way. The price of gold climbed. The international bankers met and decided that there should be two prices for gold — a world price and a price for ''qualified'' people, meaning themselves. It was ruled that no matter how high the world price of gold, they could still draw it from Fort Knox at $42.22 an ounce. The demand for Fort Knox gold continued until President Nixon stopped the practice August 15, 1971. By then most of the gold had been taken out.

In a recent newscast it was reported that there is in one New York bank vault two and a half times as much gold as there is in Fort Knox.

The International Monetary Fund

There was a meeting of international bankers. They knew that in the non-communist world there was in existence about $2,000 billion in bank-credit, and only about $45 billion in gold; thus making a 100% gold standard impossible, if they were to retain all this credit they had created out of nothing.

The international bankers came up with two ingenious devices which preserved the fetish and profit of gold for themselves while denying gold to others. The first was that ''qualified'' people, only (meaning themselves), could claim Fort Knox gold — up in price from $35 to $42.22 an ounce while the world price of gold could rise without limit.

We are here interested in the second device. It was the substitution of entries of credit in their ledgers (Paper Gold, they called it), for the metal, and granting ''Special Drawing

Rights" to use this "credit" as money, in international trade. Bankers insist that this credit be called "money," that interest be paid upon it, and that 30% of it be kept on the books as "reserve."[4]

The following is quoted from *Newsweek,* January 20, 1970, page 65.

"The world took another step away from the gold standard last week."

The occasion was the official distribution of $3.5 billion in Special Drawing Rights (S.D.R.), on the International Monetary Fund, dubbed "Paper Gold." S.D.R.'s are, in fact, a new kind of money that exists nowhere except as figures in ledgers. The United States, which receives $850 million in S.D.R.'s, didn't get so much as an engraved certificate to symbolize the fact. What's more, the S.D.R.'s are created from thin air, simply by agreement of the I.M.F., that total international reserves would be increased.[5]

In early April 1976, it was announced that the International Monetary Fund had prepared a proposal to submit to its members, to eliminate gold as international money; and to elevate their Special Drawing Right as the principal reserve in international exchange.

At this point, it is high time we ask just *what* the IMF is. Who is behind it? What philosophy is behind it?

The International Monetary Fund (IMF) was established at the Bretton Woods Conference in 1944. It was a creation of the Rockefeller interests — those who control our Federal Reserve System.

Its stated purpose was to promote foreign trade. Its apparent purpose was to force creation of United States bonds to furnish money for this Fund to lend to foreign governments. Then these governments could, in turn, pay for goods and loans furnished by factories and banks of this same financial group and the IMF.

94

Don Bell Reports, an excellent weekly newsletter (P.O. Box 2223, Palm Beach, Florida 33480), recorded a deeper and more sinister reason on October 6, 1978 — a sellout of American sovereignty as bad as the sellout of Eastern Europe at Yalta. His quote from an earlier *Dan Smoot Report* (October 21, 1963) follows:

"America is a deficit nation, which has to borrow from others on a day-to-day basis, to postpone collapse? How did this happen? It was planned at the United Nations Monetary and Financial Conference, held in Bretton Woods, New Hampshire, from July 1 to July 22, 1944. Harry Dexter White was head of the American delegation to the Bretton Woods Conference. In 1944, the United States held 60% of the world's known gold reserve, and was the dominant economic and financial power; hence, Harry Dexter White, officially designated as principal spokesman for the United States, controlled the Bretton Woods Conference. White, a member of the Council on Foreign Relations. Officially, he was Assistant Secretary of the United States Treasury; but he actually ran the Treasury Department. Henry Morganthau, Roosevelt's Secretary of Treasury, was a mere figurehead who endorsed the plans which White created, and gave White full authority to implement them. Harry Dexter White's Bretton Woods Conference of 1944 set the basic policies which our government has followed since the end of World War II. These policies were intended to accomplish four major objectives:

"1. Strip the United States of the great gold reserve by giving the gold away to other nations. . . .

"2. Build up the industrial capacity of other nations, at our expense, to eliminate American productive superiority. . . .

"3. Take world markets (and much of the American domestic market) away from American producers until capitalistic America would no longer dominate world trade. . . .

"4. Entwine American affairs — economic, political, cultural, social, educational and even religious with those of other nations, until the United States could no longer have an independent policy but would become an interdependent link in a worldwide socialist chain."

Thus we see that the pauperizing of our people and enrichment of the Rockefeller-orbit international banks has not been solely for the purpose of gaining more money.

CHAPTER 9

Other Banking Laws

Secrecy in Banking

Beginning in the war years, when Hitler sought to confiscate all Jewish wealth, Swiss banks enacted a code of secrecy. From then on we heard that American criminals used Swiss banks as depositories for their ill-gotten gains, from gambling, extortion, drug and liquor trade and prostitution — all safe from our Internal Revenue Service. At various times the I.R.S. had tried and failed to get an accounting of these deals. Finally, in January 1970, it prepared a request to Congress to intervene.

Prominent among those who flocked to the Treasury to protest this were not the expected mobsters, but, according to Jack Anderson, the executives from the Chase Manhattan Bank, Morgan Guaranty Trust Company, Manufactures Hanover, First National City and Bank of America.[1] A treaty to open these accounts in certain crimes was signed seven years later.

The bankers, and others, moved these operations. In the little village of Georgetown, capital of Grand Cayman, a tiny island south of Cuba, there are some 450 international banks. Only about two dozen of these have buildings. The rest are postal drop-boxes, administered by attorneys. The island has, also, some 4,000 international corporations.

Cayman has now agreed, as of November 1982, to open its bank deposits in investigations of crimes.

There are eighty-nine international banks in Panama. These are more formal. An ABC newscast, April 15, 1978, flashed a view of a Panama skyline showing these lofty bank buildings. Prominent among their signs was Chase Manhattan. The announcer went on to say that it is planned to make Panama the financial capital of the world.

In these havens, bankers and others may "launder" money and engage in all sorts of financial manipulations in absolute secrecy, tax free — "if profits are not brought into the United States."[1]

Liberty lobby's *The Spotlight,* December 8, 1980, states that under pressure from David and Nelson Rockefeller, the New York legislature, in 1978, passed a law endorsing the Panama type of international banks for New York City — exempting them from all taxes — and further, on November 19, 1980, the Trilateral dominated Federal Reserve Board approved such banking free-zones in New York and other states that will allow these banks. (Miami has now joined the group.)

Referring to these secret international banks, *The Spotlight* states: "They will enable American financial institutions to shed the last vestage of their national allegiance — to lend, arbitrate, exchange and manipulate their funds without regulation, restraint or concern for the future of the dollar."[2]

One day later, the New York legislature removed "all ceilings on interest rates bankers can charge their customers."

Foreign Bankers Extend Their Dominion
Into the United States

Foreigners from all over the world: France, China, England, Japan, Saudi Arabia, Brazil, West Germany, Italy and other countries are flocking into the United States to get in on our banking racket. They have bought some 77 large banks — some with capital of $10 billion or more; they have established some 150 banks. Foreign banks have 333 offices here. These banks are members of the Federal Reserve, have all its privileges, and may engage in business engaged in by American banks. Their deposits up to $100,000 may be insured by Federal Deposit Insurance — guaranteed by the American taxpayer. It is estimated that forty percent of loans made in New York are made by foreigners.

Early in July 1981, the Federal Reserve announced that it had implemented the International Banking Act of 1978. This act provides that foreign banks may have branch banks in any state, if they only accept foreign deposits of $100,000 or over. The usual reserve will not be required. It is estimated that some 150 of these branch banks will be built.

Apparently these banks may create 30 times as much as their deposits, and scatter this over the world.

The bankers' profits will be enormous, and so will the inflation.

Congress has looked with uneasiness upon this almost uncontrolled foreign entry into our finances. Nothing has been done. Congress is afraid that a move against these foreign banks, which hold some $211 billion in bank assets, would bring reprisals against United States banks which, for the bankers' own profits, have branches in foreign countries holding some $360 billion in assets.

Recently David Rockefeller said that the Chase

Manhattan Bank has branches in 125 foreign countries.

That the strewing abroad of great amounts of Federal Reserve bank-credit by our financiers, and under their direction, by our profligate government, is dangerous, may be seen by the way this money is coming back to us. The *U.S. News and World Report,* August 14, 1972, page 53, states:

"The United States, long the world's greatest creditor nation, now finds itself borrowing billions of dollars from foreign countries to pay for burgeoning government outlays at home. . . . Last year alone, these foreign government banks provided almost four-fifths of additional funds the Treasury was forced to borrow." As a result, this country is in hock to official agencies of other nations for something like 49 billion dollars. By now, the debt must be very large; American taxpayers are borrowing and paying interest to foreigners for money to run our government. At the same time, we are sending billions of dollars to arm and develop Israel to develop Russia; and to keep the dictators in power. It is estimated that almost 60 percent of our dollars are in foreign hands.

With this money foreigners are buying not so much our products as our country. They are buying the United States. They are buying United States bonds and stock on the New York Stock Exchange. They are buying homes, apartment buildings, hotels — $100 million in one deal. An aerial view of an Italian plant in the north looks almost like the Pentagon. The Japanese are building factories all over America. Their goods will not be stamped "made in Japan." They will be made in Japanese factories in America.

It is estimated that foreign companies have partial or complete ownership of over 1,000 companies in the United States. From these companies come products bearing brand names bought by most Americans. Volkswagen, Honda, and Renault cars are built here.

In the first week of October 1982, an ABC newscast announced that Secretary Watt seeks to lease to Kuwait, oil and mineral rights on Western North Carolina government land.

A shocking article on foreign ownership in America is carried in the December 6, 1982, edition of *U.S. News & World Report*. It states that foreigners now have $100 billion in investments here, and also hold $250 billion in stocks and government bonds, and other bonds.

Foreigners are buying great areas of our finest land, now tens of thousands of rich farmland in eastern North Carolina. "Open Grounds Farms" in Carteret County consist of 45,000 acres. It is Italian owned. A Japanese farm, "The Shima American" in Washington County has 7,000 acres. "The First Colony Farms" in Washington, Terrel, Hyde and Dale Counties consist of some 380,000 acres. It is said to be owned by Malcome McLean of New Jersey; and said again that foreign money is behind it. It is certainly not owned by North Carolina farmers. Foreigners are buying the finest land in Texas, Louisiana, Kansas, Mississippi — all over the nation. In the winter of 1978 an Arabian agent walked over the snow in Killitas County, Washington, and came away with a deed for 25,663 acres. Total acreage in foreign hands is now nearing twelve million acres.

(Outside the small clique that operates our monetary system, few of our citizens can build factories. Impoverished native farmers, our finest citizens, cannot buy these farms. Many cannot hold what they have.)

"In January 1983 over 200 farmers had stormed the courthouse in Springfield, Colorado, demanding that farm foreclosures be stopped . . . (according to AP) 'Fifty percent of the farmers in Michigan are in trouble. . . .'

"But to say that *all* owners of farms and *all* bankers are

101

in trouble is to miss the point. It is the smaller, community bank that is in danger of closing, and the independent family farmer who fears foreclosure" *(Don Bell Reports,* January 14, 1983).

House Bails Out Big Banks

This article by Congressman Ron Paul from Texas, in *The Spotlight* for June 8, 1981, states that the House Banking Committee voted $13 billion to the World Bank affiliates, the International Development Association and the Latin American, Asian and African development banks. Mr. Paul said: "It works like this: money goes from the American taxpayer to the World Bank, to the borrowing countries, to big U.S. Banks — all under the heading of helping the poor."

He ends with, "It's time to quit giving welfare to the powerful and the wealthy."

The *U.S. News & World Report,* for August 10, 1981, stated that the government will "provide foreign governments and buyers with $5.06 billion . . . to purchase expensive U.S. exports."

David Stockman has shown *(Reader's Digest,* August 1981), that all the billions of dollars the United States has contributed to the Export-Import Bank, "has benefited only a handful of huge corporations."

On Groundhog Day, February 2, 1982, it was announced that the United States paid $120 million on the interest of Poland's debts: "To keep Poland from default." (And, of course, to save the banks and give them their profits.)

A little later the United States paid communist Romania's interest.

102

The Money Market Fund

Bankers started the Money Market Fund around 1921, and have gradually developed it into what it is today. On its face it is a program for the little man. Its real benefit is to the bankers. To them it is an open door into the nation's wealth.

In this program the government lends money to students, farmers, small businessmen, house builders and others. (The government has loaned to students for the past 25 years. There are now three million students receiving these loans.)

The money is loaned in two ways: first a loan at the interest the government must pay to get the money — say, 15 percent. If and when such loans are defaulted, the government loses. The second way is by a loan subsidy. Here the government pays seven percent of the interest and charges the borrower eight percent.

The government gets this money by selling short-term Treasury notes carrying, say, 15 percent interest.

This program puts the government into a position of making a great many shaky, questionable loans — loans which are in reality indirect commercial bank loans — to people the banks would not lend to.

The banks, indirectly making the loans and reaping the benefits, are safe. The banks get this money by offering, say, 14.16 percent on time deposits in $10,000 units.

At first glance one might think that the bankers made a profit of only .84 percent. The banks are, however, not out for trifles. As this is a time deposit, as it all goes to one place, and as the government will promptly pay the principal and interest, by borrowing again, bankers can safely do what the ancient goldsmiths did. They put the $10,000 deposit in reserve, and on their computers, create thirty times this amount of money ($3,000,000), and buy Treasury Notes upon which the government pays 15 percent interest, or $45,000 a year (this figure varies). The bank pays its depositor $1,416. Discounting for time lag, it seems that the bank could receive as much as $40,000 a year gross profit on that one deposit.

Total government involvement in the Money Market Fund has been estimated to be about $1 trillion.

But for all this bankers have been restive. They have not received all the profit. Relatively few bank accounts reached the $10,000 unit required for the purchase of a government security. Other financiers, seeing the opportunity, created Mutual Funds, to overcome this restriction. These Mutual Funds advertised for and collected smaller amounts, which, added together, reached the required units — each small depositor being paid his proportional share of the large interest.

Super Now Accounts

On December 14, 1982, almost all restrictions were lifted from bankers in their efforts to recover a part of the $231 billion Money Market funds which had been taken over by Mutual Funds. Checking accounts of $2,500 now qualify for unlimited interest.

There is feverish activity among the bankers. Some banks have offered $100 prizes for such deposits. Some banks have offered as much as 25 percent interest, and unlimited checking.

Financial Giants Consolidate Vast Money Spectrum

This is the headline of an important article by Tracy Ehre in Liberty Lobby's *Spotlight* of July 23, 1981.

The Prudential Life Insurance Company (having a $60 billion investment portfolio), is acquiring Bache Group, the nation's sixth largest brokerage house. The American Express, insurance conglomerate and largest credit card issuer, is buying Shearson, Loch Rhodes, Wall Street's second largest brokerage firm. Sears Roebuck and Company, the nation's largest retailer, owner of Allstate Insurance Company, and number one in providing consumer installment credit, has bought Dean Witter Reynolds, Inc., the nation's fifth largest security firm — and also Coldwell Banker and Company, the nation's leading independent real estate broker.

The purpose of all this is to establish a new financial system furnishing every related facility — credit cards, insurance, investments, loans and checking accounts outside the control of the Federal Reserve or any other restraint.

Seeing this, the great commercial banks are pressing for new rules which would free them from regulations.

This trend, says *Spotlight*, ''Will ultimately include a national banking system under which profits will be neatly divided among a handful of superbanks and super-conglomerates, all controlled by the same clique of financiers who have schemed for years toward this end.''[3]

Finance, the manipulation and lending of money, has become the world's greatest business. This book will show that it should be the smallest.

Depository Institutions Deregulation and Monetary Control Act of 1980

This public law 96-221, March 31, 1980, is an amendment to the Federal Reserve Act of 1913. It consists of sixty-one pages of fine print. Its purported purpose is to eliminate the limiting of interest rates which may be paid on

105

deposits, "... and other purposes." There are many changes. The reader is given 130 U.S.C. reference numbers which would have to be looked up if some passages are to be at all clear. The bill grants many prerogatives to the Board of Governors of the Federal Reserve System. These prerogatives include the power to alter numerous regulations concerning the operations of banks and saving and loan institutions, and also gives them the power to monetize foreign debts.

The gist of the foreign debt amendment is copied as follows: "... insert or other depository institutions," and "as the Board determines," and "as the Board may deem appropriate." The second paragraph of section 16 of the Federal Reserve Act (12 U.S.C. 412) is amended

A. by inserting before the period at the end of the third sentence the following: "or assets that Federal Reserve banks may purchase or hold under section 14 of this Act," and

B. by adding to the end thereof the following: "collateral shall not be required for Federal Reserve notes which are held in the vaults of Federal Reserve banks."

Section 14(bxl) of the Federal Reserve Act — is amended by inserting after "reclamation districts," the following: "and obligations of, or fully guaranteed as to principal and interest by a foreign government or agency thereof."

These few words carry a wide world of meaning and danger.

The bankers, of course, have their interpretation and reasons for the law. Paul Volcker, Chairman of the Federal Reserve, said the intent was to include foreign government securities as eligible for purchase by the Fed, so that the Fed can invest its non-interest bearing foreign currencies in interest-bearing obligations. How the Federal Reserve happens to have this foreign money isn't told.

Several things stand out.

There is no limit on the interest that banks can demand on the money they lend.

Notice the wide, unlimited powers given to the operators of the Federal Reserve.

With authority given by paragraph "A," the Federal Reserve may use the money and credit of our people to buy uncollectable notes held by huge New York banks. These banks loaned the money, deposited by Arabs and others, to communist countries, dictators in other countries, and to shaky governments in Africa, Asia and South America. The amounts of the loans are estimated to be near $850 billion.

Paragraph "B" means that these foreign notes are unsecured, that there is no guarantee that these notes will be paid, that their payment depends upon the promise — the word "guarantee," given by some country or its agent. The banks couldn't collect these loans, there is not the slightest hope that they will ever be paid; either principal or interest.

The United States has paid, to bankers, the defaulted interest on loans to Poland and Romania. (They will·soon be due again.) On President Reagan's trip to South America he pledged a billion dollar "loan" to Brazil, . . . to help that nation meet its massive interest payments to international lenders. (This money is for the great New York bankers.)

Real fangs have been given the IMF and the Fed by the Monetary Control Act of 1980. A letter by Congressman Ron Paul (R-TX), published in the *Don Bell Report* (September 17, 1982), shows how the Fed is now monetizing the bad debts of the Third World and the Communist countries:

> "The imminent or present bankruptcies of Mexico, Argentina, Bolivia, and Poland ought to direct our attention to the Monetary Control Act once

again.

"By the end of August, the Federal Reserve had purchased debts of West Germany, Switzerland, Italy, Canada, France, and England, and used those debts as collateral for printing and issueing, on 70 different occasions, about $2 billion worth of Federal Reserve notes from four different Reserve Banks.

"There is no legal impediment that would prevent the Federal Reserve from buying the debts of Mexico, Argentina, Bolivia, or Poland and using them for the same purpose. With the nationalization of the banks in Mexico, virtually all Mexican debt becomes eligible for Fed purchase, for the Monetary Control Act empowers the Fed to buy the debts issued or guaranteed by foreign governments or their agents.

"Mexico's external debt is between $80-85 billion, $27 billion of which comes due this year. Mexico has already announced its inability to pay, and Argentina has requested a standby IMF loan. The Federal Reserve, which prides itself on its lender-of-last-resort position, will be bailing out the world.

"The total Communist and Third World external debt is now about $850 billion. In the next few weeks, the Monetary Control Act will become more and more important.

"Sincerely,

Ron Paul, Member of Congress"

This mixing of our money with all others is but a step toward the goal of the internationalist — the destruction of this country's integrity.

Propaganda for full use of this Bill has begun.

As the Arabians advanced the price of oil from $1.10 to

$32.00 a barrel, an enormous amount of money was credited to them. They did not lend this money themselves. They deposited it in great western banks, at interest. The bankers, hoping for billions of dollars profit, loaned the money, unsecured, to governments and individuals in communist countries, those ruled by dictators, and undeveloped countries.

These debtors cannot, or will not pay.

We are now told that a sharp drop in the price of oil would be calamitous; that the Arabians might call for their money; that the banks would be unable to pay, and that the American people would have to put up the money. It is further stated that if the people did not pay, the bankers would go broke, and that there would be a terrible, worldwide depression.

Our people paid for this oil once. They should not pay again and again — with profits to bankers.

The limit on our government's bank deposit insurance is $100,000 on each account, though some accounts may be many billions. The insured amount is the extent of our responsibility.

CHAPTER 10

The Federal Reserve as It Is Today

My presentation of the Federal Reserve and the diagram, made about 1974, are still helpful to those who would understand the system. They are still true, but amendment after amendment since then has carried the system far beyond that. The act is now totally obscure.

In 1933 the Honorable Louis T. McFadden, Chairman of the Banking and Currency Committee, United States Congress, said:

"Every effort has been made by the Fed (the Federal Reserve System) to conceal its powers, but the truth is the Fed has usurped the government. It controls everything here and it controls all our foreign relations. It makes and breaks governments at will."

If there was any doubt of this then, there can be no doubt now. The Federal Reserve has ultimate control of all the wealth of this nation, and those bankers who control the system use it as their own personal tool to enrich themselves at the expense of the nation.

The kind of stability the Federal Reserve provides is all too well known. As the debt-laden economy falters, the remedy has been to put more money into circulation by making larger loans. This, together with accumulating interest, brings on inflation. To check inflation, interest is raised and money withheld, throwing millions of people out of work, and thousands of businesses into bankruptcy.

A tabulation of nine of these oscillations, some violent, may be read in the *U.S. News & World Report* for February 2, 1970. There have been several since then — the worst in 1982. Formerly recessions came about once in every seven years — now every three or four years.

Great financiers and their experts know how to take advantage of these dips in the economy. The outpouring of government bonds are gobbled up at once, and eyes turned toward the next issue.

Our Present Depression

The value of our dollar steadily shrinks. Franz Pick, publisher of *World Currency,* stated that the 1976 dollar had the purchasing power of 12 cents of the 1940 dollar. Today the estimate is about eight cents or less.

By June 1981 the interest rate had reached 21 percent. President Reagan and members of Congress appealed to Paul Volcker, Chairman of the Federal Reserve, to lower the interest rate. Mr. Volcker, sure of himself and his power, smilingly refused. The withholding of money brought on a steady decline in the economy. There was no money to buy cars, and the factories curtailed or stopped production. Furniture factories, textile plants, steel mills, and hundreds of other types of factories closed. Millions of workers were laid off to apply for unemployment insurance — a drain on the government and therefore on the taxpayer. Home building all but stopped. Real estate could not be sold. By November 1981, a real depression had set in.

History is repeating itself. The Federal Reserve is again withholding money — the very life blood of the economy. And, as our present depression deepens, voices are raised against President Reagan and his hopeless attempt to balance the budget. Our welfare system is blamed, labor unions — oil.

No, it is not these that have brought this about. These are but a recent, small part of it.

We are now in a deepening depression. More than 12 million people are out of work. Many more have given up and are not listed. Many of the unemployed cannot pay mortgage charges and are evicted. Tens of thousands are homeless. Many are hungry and cold. Those who cannot be accommodated in charitable homes are forced to sleep on park benches or on the streets. Each morning large city authorities gather up those who froze in the night.

The meaning of all this may be outlined in one paragraph.

Bankers have used the Federal Reserve to strip this nation of its wealth. Much of this has been scattered over the world. Top financiers and industrialists, bent on controlling our government and internationalizing our nation, formed the Council on Foreign Relations and the Trilateral Commission. They have taken in politicians they can use. With enormous bank rolls they elect our President, who then appoints, from elitist members, the top executive branch of our government. They pay much of the election expenses of Congressmen. Any law the leaders of these groups request is passed. The nation's natural resources have been given away. The industrialists, in search of more profit, have moved their factories to foreign countries where labor is cheap, where they are free from labor unions, regulations, and taxes of our government. To bring their foreign-made goods duty-free, they have had our President enter unfair trade agreements that have flooded this country with foreign goods. All this has turned millions of persons adrift. The very wealthy pay comparatively little taxes — these wrung from those below. The welfare burden for the dispossessed is thus shifted onto the backs of the middle class. Beset with high taxes and high prices, they are rapidly losing what little possessions they have.

The Office of Management and Budget reported that Federal borrowing soaked up more than half of all credit available in the United States in 1982. The reason for this is the hemorrhaging interest on the national debt, now totally out of control. Don Bell made it perfectly clear in a recent report (December 3, 1982), quoted here, in part.

"The Census Bureau and the Commerce Department have recently issued a report stating that for the first time, receipts and spending by all forms of government in the United States both exceeded $1 trillion in fiscal year 1980-81. And debt also grew to $1.4 trillion. These, remember, are figures compiled by appointed government bureaucrats, and the figures don't tell the whole story. A more recent description of the situation is shown in the statement of account recently published by the National Taxpayers Union, and shown below. The amounts boggle the mind, but they do reveal that we are in serious trouble as a nation. A private economist recently pointed out that between 1972 and 1981, the federal government had to borrow $400 biilion to pay all its bills. Between 1981 and 1982, the national debt increased another $320 billion. By September 30, 1983, there will be an ad-

114

ditional $400 billion in federal and federal-sponsored borrowing. This means that the total amount borrowed between February 1981 and September 30, 1983, will be a whopping $729 billion — and that doesn't include loans made to foreign countries nor to major private corporations. When these figures are included, says the economist, the total amount of federal, federal-sponsored and private borrowing could total over $1 trillion; most of which will be added to our present public debt of $1.4 trillion.''

DEBT OR LIABILITY ITEM	GROSS COST	YOUR SHARE
Public Debt	$ 1,050,000,000,000	$ 13,125
Accounts Payable	$ 167,000,000,000	$ 2.088
Undelivered Orders	$ 487,000,000,000	$ 6,088
Long Term Contracts	$ 21,000,000,000	$ 263
Loan and Credit Guarantees	$ 360,000,000,000	$ 4,500
Insurance Commitments	$ 2,227,000,000,000	$ 27,838
Annuity Programs	$ 7,281,000,000,000	$ 91,013
Unadjudicated Claims International Commitments & other Financial Obligations	$ 59,000,000,000	$ 738
TOTAL	$11,652,000,000,000	$145,653

Interest on these debts is many hundred billion dollars a year. This interest, this unearned claim for wealth, this addition to our monetary system, is the main cause of inflation.

The creation and handling of money, which should be the simplest and most helpful of operations, has become the greatest business and the most oppressive one. The buildings of financial centers tower over all others.

CHAPTER 11

The Search for Relief

In view of our failing economy and dire prophecies, our people are uneasy. Many are deeply disturbed. All over the country there are calls to abolish the Federal Reserve. Many people are considering ways of survival in the event of a collapse of the monetary system.

For thousands of years, gold was used as the most trusted medium of exchange in three-way barter. Later it was used and thought of as the only true money — something material, having intrinsic value in itself. Because of this, many people are buying gold and storing it in select depositories, or burying it in jars in the ground. (And well they might — there will be a collapse, not only of paper money, but of our entire economic system, if the men who control these are left in charge.) With no issue of United States gold coins, the people have been buying Krugerrands from South America and gold coins minted in Canada or Mexico.

Daniel Rosenthal's December 1982 *Silver and Gold Report* features Dr. Franz Pick, internationally known currency expert. Pick says private gold hoarding now absorbs

117

almost 25 percent of the entire Free World gold production. ''The total private worldwide hoards of gold in 1982 amounted to about 26,250 metric tons in all.''

This current movement among our patriots is accompanied by a strong move to require our government to abolish the Federal Reserve, and produce gold coins that they can buy.

Congressman Ron Paul has introduced a bill in the Congress to abolish the Federal Reserve. He and others favor a return to a gold standard, and he also intends to legalize U.S. government minting of gold coins.

Many thoughts arise.

We must remember that in times of the early goldsmiths, with their 100 percent gold reserve, people rarely used gold coins as money. There were related dangers and inconvenience in its use. People used the goldsmith's receipts as paper money.

If this nation went on a gold standard with gold valued at $500 an ounce (or much higher if the financiers can drive it up before that time), it is inconceivable that the nation would take one five-hundreds of an ounce of gold and with it coin a dollar, nor would it be possible to thus produce a five-dollar coin or a ten or a twenty. Except for a few people who might want to possess gold, the nation's gold would lie in a vault at Fort Knox, and we would still use paper money.

(We did have silver coins. Then these were discontinued.)

It is very unlikely that, ever again, will we have widely circulating coins of intrinsic value.

If our monetary system were made sound, it would make no difference what we use for currency — means to keep the records for small transactions.

The idea that a gold standard would limit the amount of money that could be issued is unfounded in fact. The amount of money issued depends upon the character of the men in charge of the system, not on hard money backing. With brief lapses, this nation was on the gold standard from the time of its founding until 1933. Never did the gold standard prevent wide gyrations in the economy. With enormous amounts of gold in our Treasury there was the wild inflation of the mid-twenties.

It is improbable that this nation would ever return to a 100-percent gold standard. Under a fractional reserve system there would be rules which could be varied. An ounce of gold could be set as the basis of $500 or it could be $5,000.

In my own memory we were on the gold standard during the Cleveland panic, the panic of 1907, and the great depression of the early thirties.

In 1933, in the great depression, caused by those in charge of the Federal Reserve system, almost all the gold in this nation was taken from the people under threats of a $10,000 fine and a five-year term in the penitentiary. Most of the gold was then taken over by New York banks — interest charges and other manipulations of our monetary system furnishing the money. The price they paid was small; in the long view they got the gold for nothing. These bankers, and successors of the same ilk, have held the gold in their vaults awaiting the day when they can dupe the people and dispose of it at great profit. The gold has been stored without interest. The bankers have no use for it. They can't sell it except to each other. (This probably determines the price.) Time is passing. Some bankers are restless. They are pressing for a return to a gold standard in our monetary system, and thus force the government to buy, or to monetize the gold. Other bankers with large holdings of gold are biding their time. They control the Federal Reserve, and have a better idea. When they have made all paper money and the money it represents worthless, these bankers will then use their gold as money, to acquire almost unlimited wealth.

Nowhere are we told how the bankers left in charge can be prevented from perverting and destroying a new gold standard system, as they perverted and destroyed the old one. What is to prevent them from taking the gold again?

Those people who have been influenced by the banker's propaganda are helping them by advocating a return to a gold standard. They should consider well the plain consequences of such a move. This becomes apparent in the answers to one simple question.

Just how will the nation go on a gold standard?

Is it proposed that the government buy the bankers' gold at an enormous profit to them? If so, how will we pay for it? Shall we issue bonds and go into debt, and through an enormous increase in taxes, pay to bankers interest on the gold? If so, we may suffer the resulting loss of homes and businesses — adding millions of people to our welfare rolls. The money given to the bankers, along with increased taxes, would jeopardize every home in the nation. Or again, is it proposed that the government (the people) surrender all government-owned land, along with its enormous wealth of natural resources?

Another alternative may be envisioned: for the nation to return to a gold standard with what little gold remains in Fort Knox and, as Ron Paul suggests in his *Gold, Peace and Prosperity,* page 44, return to Free Market Money. This means that we monetize gold and then allow the bankers to coin their own tremendous hoard, tens of thousands of tons of ill-gotten gold. This is not a free market, with the price of gold set each morning by dignitaries in London!

Either of these courses would give the bankers hundreds of billions of dollars

Even with the final end of fiat money and all currency

120

now anchored to gold, would it work? Would real freedom for the nation result, or would the gold hoard in the vault beneath the Chase Manhattan Bank, reportedly larger than that in Fort Knox, seal our people into slavery to its owners?

The Rothschilds of Europe are known to favor a gold standard, while the Rockefellers reportedly favor the cashless, fiat ''Special Drawing Rights'' advocated in their IMF-World Bank schemes. If most of this hoarded gold mentioned by Dr. Pick is actually owned by such international banking families, how can the world or this nation ever break free from their control by anchoring all money to what they have?

The financiers who now use the Federal Reserve System as their own private mint have used secrecy, hundreds of obscure amendments, propaganda and threats in the wrecking of our economy. They now threaten that if the government does not pay their defaulting foreign loans, with interest, they will go broke and civilization will go down with them. In full control of our monetary system, these men are creating dollars, indirectly paying themselves, and adding these foreign debts to the United States debt.

All of this has so confused the issue of money that many people feel that an understanding of money is beyond their comprehension, and do not want to become involved.

This is a mistake. The creation and use of money in its pure form is simple. People can understand it. We must face up to this all-important issue.

We now come to the heart of this book.

CHAPTER 12

A New Monetary System

The Money Changers

Oppression by money changers is as old as history.

No monetary system will save the nation if the present financiers, their ilk, and their paid government officials remain in charge. All of these, along with the monetary system they created, must be swept away for a new start.

Clearly these secular matters are related to spiritual ones.

> "Jesus went up to the temple . . . and He made a scourge of cords, and cast all out of the temple . . . and He poured out the changers' money, and overthrew their tables" (John 2:15).

All who believe in Him should unite and follow His example.

It is here proposed:

- That, by our vote, we abolish the Federal Reserve, and free our monetary system from those men who have operated it, and established a new system, run by honest men, not for their own personal gain, but for the benefit of the nation — and thus for every citizen alike.

- That never again will the nation, for the very privilege of existing, issue bonds, to be placed in a privately controlled monetary system, to be drawn out by bankers — who then receive, yearly, hundreds of billions of dollars — paid by our taxpayers.

- That the nation create its own money — and from it pay its own reduced expenses and lend it to our people at interest.

- That all this money be recollected and reissued. That all interest on the loan of its money come to the nation to reduce taxes.

- That that interest be canceled as it is paid in, and never again be given for nothing to a few financiers with which to lay claim on, and to buy unearned wealth — the main cause of inflation.

Playing-Card Money
A Monetary System that Belonged to the People

The early French-Canadian Colony had no money to pay its troops. The expected ships did not come. Time passed. The situation became desperate.

The colony's governor, in 1685, made the colony's own money. He requisitioned all playing cards. Using whole cards for coins of high monetary value and pieces of cards for smaller coins, he wrote upon each its arbitrary value and on each wrote his name. The governor decreed that this playing-card money should be accepted as full legal tender.

The money could not be counterfeited. It was first issued

to pay the troops, and was then issued for other government expenses. Its amount was carefully controlled. It was accepted for taxes, and then reissued.

This improvised money was accepted at once. When the people realized this perfectly good money came to them without taxation at its source, it became very popular.

French kings came and went. Each tried to suppress the playing-card money and lend his own, but the people would not give up their money. As cards became worn, they were replaced. Additional issues were made when the need arose.

The playing-card money was the main Canadian money for the better part of 80 years. Its fate was sealed when in 1763 the Treaty of Paris gave Canada to England.

The Plymouth Socialist Experiment

The Plymouth Colony was first organized on a communal basis. All food and other products of labor were brought to a common storehouse, and all members of the colony alike drew from the store. Taking advantage of this, freeloaders lived on the labor of the industrious. William Bradford was elected governor in 1621, and with gaps between terms, served in that capacity until his death in 1657. He saved the colony from socialist ruin when he assigned families to lands — to either produce for themselves or starve. The colony learned its lesson.

The Massachusetts Note

The Puritans, in 1692, eighty-two years before the Revolutionary War, while their religious fervor, their search for freedom and for truth still flared brightly, rebelled against the injustices of the English, gold-standard monetary system. Pat Brooks in *The Return of the Puritans,* states:

"The Puritan era produced generations of thinkers who were able to live for lofty goals because they were fed in the spirit of God's Word." They developed a nearly perfect monetary system.

The colony printed and controlled its own unbacked legal tender notes. The notes were used for government expenses and development, without payment to anyone. The notes were recollected through taxation, and reissued. Large amounts of notes were loaned, well secured, at interest. This interest coming to the colony, greatly reduced taxes. Nothing could have been simpler. There was unrivaled prosperity. Expert economists had no part there. The system came spontaneously from purity of heart and common sense. The English king repressed it.

The United States Note

Abraham Lincoln fought for an honest money. In the throes of the Civil War he persuaded Congress to issue the United States Note. In this way he avoided paying bankers huge interest rates they wanted to lend their notes to the government.

Lincoln then attempted to make the note full legal tender. He was thwarted by the bankers and their "experts." They saw to it that the Lincoln "greenback" carried this statement: "The United States will pay to bearer $1 at the Treasury in New York." This inferred that the United States Note was not real money. There were also exceptions. The note could not be used as payment of interest on the public debt, nor for import fees.

Yet the United States Notes helped save the Union. They served as money for a hundred years without any cost save their printing. They saved the nation many millions of dollars of interest. The government was not allowed to get

126

any interest the notes earned, however. The bankers got that.

Many writers, discrediting unsecured legal tender notes, fail to tell the complete story. The United States Note was the first note issued by the government. As explained earlier, the note, when issued, had no backing. The bankers made a business of depreciating it. Among the 7,000 different kinds of other bank notes, the United States Note was the only one that bore exceptions limiting its use. Yet, like the others, it said ''payable on demand'' on its face.

Even though United States Notes decreased in value after the Civil War, they survived the big change in currency at the turn of the century. Critics do not tell us that after the year 1900, when Congress required all American money to be maintained at par with gold, the United States Note was invincible. This unsecured note, with all its exceptions, remained at par with gold until gold was removed in 1933. Afterwards it continued at par with all other United States money until the present day.

In 1963 United States Notes were made full legal tender. Though rare, these notes are *still* full legal tender, in circulation and in use today, and still maintain their full purchasing power.

I propose that when the Federal Reserve Act of 1913 is repealed, these United States Notes be simply increased as our only paper money. Furthermore, I propose that they should be used as the Massachusetts notes were used by the Puritans.

Modern Money

Modern money is, and should be, nothing but bookkeeping — a record of Federal indebtedness (tax-credit) which serves as our medium of exchange. As amounts of currency

127

(the rapid part of the stream), pennies, dimes, quarters and dollar bills, we carry in our pockets, pass from person to person, they keep an accurate account of trifling amounts of tax-credit the Federal government owes its holders. Other records are kept in banks. Most money has never existed save as credits in computers.

With a computer a trifling amount of money or billions of dollars may be created, credited, debited, transferred, safely stored or obliterated in a few minutes time at practically no cost. That is the right way to operate a monetary system.

The only question is: who will keep the books, and reap its enormous profit, a few bankers or the people?

A Change of Direction

This nation desperately needs a new monetary system. To get it won't be easy.

The great financiers who control this nation are not satisfied with the wealth they have — they want it all. They haven't the slightest idea of giving up their racket. They will never relent. They will try ridicule. They will cry socialism, communism; spend billions on propaganda; fight; stop at nothing to retain and further their favored position. Anything and everything they will do but get off our backs.

A determined effort of voters, at the polls, can pull them off.

In Conclusion

The people, after all, are the real rulers of this nation. We can no longer permit the bankers the privilege of creating the nation's money, taking what they will, and dictating every important policy.

The fundamentals of money; used not to pile up wealth,

but as a standard of value and a medium of exchange — a flux to flow through and bond various parts, of say a house, together, can be understood by everyone. And everyone should, as his Constitutional right, share in its management and its bounty.

The proposed reforms are not only logical, they are based upon an inherent sense of right and wrong. They will not, however, come by themselves, nor can we rely upon isolated and sporadic action. The movement to gain this end must be determined, well organized, and far-reaching.

THE VOTE IS THE THING.

CHAPTER 13

Regaining Control
of Our Government

We are prone to think that to accomplish any mean-
ingful reform we must gain the presidency. This is a mistake.

To begin with, it is now next to impossible to elect a
third party President. The two leading political parties have,
through legislative action, assured themselves a place on the
Presidential ballot, and have made it impossible for a third
party candidate to fulfill the maze of requirements and start
on an equal footing. Presidential candidates of the major parties have access to Federal campaign funds, the backing of
great banks and other corporations, the support of many
already in office, and television and newspaper coverage; all
denied to newcomers.

And even if this third party candidate should be elected
president he could, as an isolated reformer, accomplish little
or nothing.

The President is a foreign nation negotiator, an advisor,
and an executive charged with carrying out laws passed by
Congress. Bureaucrats stall and ignore his orders. The
Supreme Court may overrule him. Congress may reverse his

actions or may refuse to follow his recommendations.

New leaders seeking reform should forego, at least for the present, all personal ambition. They should not divide those who wish a change into ineffectual factions and political parties. They should join forces and work for a real reform.

Reform must start at the grass roots — as dry as tender from long abuse by financiers and politicians.

Scattered throughout the United States are men who know and ponder much that is said in this book. You may know them by their occasional letters in local newspapers. These are the men to spark a true reform. They could succeed if one of them in each Congressional District would ferret out the others; induce them to read this book and to come together at his house — there to talk of these things, and, uniting, form a nucleus for action.

Each of these men should then go out among their friends and neighbors with the word.

They should form the Independent Voters Party — that is, they should as a group — vote for converted candidates of any party.

Don't let anyone tell you that we need experienced federal officials — meaning the same old crowd. Some 5,000 Super Bureaucrats run the government. What is needed is elected officials with common sense, a sense of fairness, of honor and a love of their country.

The first office to control is that of U.S. representative — the local one — filled every two years. If the incumbant, be he Republican or Democrat, is acceptable as to moral character and is intelligent, he should be approached and asked to read this book, and to publically swear that he will use his office in a continuous attempt to inaugurate these recommended reforms. If he agrees to this the group as a body should vote for him.

If he will not agree to this, the group should offer their support, under the same terms, to the candidate of the other chief political party. Failing here, they should nominate a candidate from their own group — under the same stipulations.

This playing in and out of the present political parties would soon have its local effect. Then upon a coming together of all the states' Congressional groups, the Senate elections could be controlled, and after that the union of all groups would control the Presidency.

The key to success will depend upon the selfless patriotic effort of those who lead this movement. Hundreds of thousands of our finest young men have died in senseless wars. Surely here there are those who will put forth the effort to stop wars and enact reforms, sorely needed, and which promise so much.

The story as told in this book cannot be convincingly told in brief political campaigns. It must be read. It must be told in letters to the newspapers, in meetings in halls — and on the street — year in and year out.

Once patriotism and the determination to throw off oppressive rule swept through this country with an almost religious fervor. It should again. The *Declaration of Independence* and *Constitution* should be reprinted and circulated throughout the land; everyone who loves his country should sign it and do his part.

Nationalization of Our Monetary System

The *Declaration of Independence* declares the equal rights of man; that no man shall be given, by law, an advantage over other men. Our concern here is the gift of the nation's monetary system to financiers. The *Constitution* provides in Article I, Section 8, paragraph 5:

"Congress shall have power to coin money and regulate the value thereof and of foreign coin."

This provision was regarded as of supreme importance. (The provision for Freedom of Speech which the press so fiercely guards was an afterthought — an amendment.)

For those who might think that the words, "Shall have power," does not necessarily mean that Congress shall exercise that power, we quote from the same section of the Constitution — Section 8:

"Congress shall have power

"To lay and collect taxes . . .

"To coin money . . .

"To declare war. . . ."

Congress and Congress alone should exercise these "powers." It is not implied that Congress has a right to delegate any of these powers to anyone.

In Clause 18 of the same section, the Constitution provides that Congress shall have the "power to make all laws which shall be necessary and proper for carrying into execution the foregoing power."

In case after case the Supreme Court has upheld the proposition that "whatever power there is over the currency is vested in Congress."[1]

"In the 1870's the Supreme Court held that Congress has the power to determine what shall be 'Legal Tender'; to make currency (that is, the United States Note) legal tender, even though in doing so Congress overturned private contracts that had been entered into before the law was passed. After Congress passed the Legal Tender Act, creditors were required to accept paper money (The United States Note) in settlement of debts for which there were contracts calling for payments in gold."[2] This Supreme Court decision was also the basis for confiscation of the peoples' gold, December 28, 1933.

Individuals were even forbidden to own gold bullion, the then declared basis of the country's money. For this they were paid in paper money at $20.67 an ounce, raised to $35.00 an ounce January 15, 1934.

In short, Congressional power extends to and over all our money, its reserves and its control — no private individuals or corporations has a claim here. It is not necessary to consult with bankers.

The fact that foreign investors own and are operating banks all over our nation does not change this. The U.S. *Constitution* asserts that Congress has power over foreign coins that happen to be here. It certainly has power over foreign banks located here using our money to drain this nation of its wealth. When these foreign banks are taken over, foreign governments will mount reprisals against our great banks which have established foreign branches and are busy exploiting the people of these lands. Let them. Such operations are motivated by pure greed. The United States of America must make a bold stroke soon or be totally engulfed.

Congress must implement its power and provide the nation with a cheap and sure medium of exchange. It must also assert its absolute control over each and every financial institution that handles money. And it must give all benefits of the system to the people.

When Congress begins a real reform, the bankers, with their army of lawyers, might try to persuade the Supreme Court that bankers have a vested interest in their racket; that the ramifications of their system are too deeply rooted to be disturbed; that Congress has, by inaction, lost the power to repeal the Federal Reserve Act, and to make other reforms; the bankers are being deprived of their property without ''due process'' and all that.

If this should be attempted, Congress should rule that

135

this case is beyond the Court's jurisdiction. Grounds for this is found in Article 3, Section 2, of the United States Constitution, which reads: ''. . . The Supreme Court shall have Appellate jurisdiction both as to law and as to fact, with such exceptions and under such regulations as Congress shall make.''

Historically and by Constitutional Law, the nation's money and the benefits of its issue belong to the people.

The time for action is long overdue. Evolution of the money and banking system has dispelled the problems Lincoln faced. These matters are now handled with paper and ink.

We must return to the monetary system inaugurated by Massachusetts in 1692. By this return, we mean a full and absolute reform.

The First Step

We must repeal the Federal Reserve Act of 1913, together with its amendments and all banking laws that conflict with the new monetary system.

This would end the term of office of every Federal Reserve official. The last line of the original act (1913) provides for this repeal. The act also gives the sole condition for this — that is, the return to the bankers the amount of money they first subscribed — approximately $1 billion (such a reserve is being held in the Federal Reserve banks, earmarked for this purpose).

Establish under Congressional control an organization to take over all assets of the Federal Reserve System. Change its name to ''The United States Treasury Department of Money,'' and the names of its branches to the United States Treasury Banks of their respective cities of location.

The new system shall continue, without interruption,

the function of creating and supplying money to the nation. The United States of America's dollar shall be its unit; its value shall be controlled by Congress.

The creation of this nation's money shall be in these United States Treasury Banks and nowhere else. Its method of production shall be by entries of government indebtedness in their ledgers or upon their computers, and a corresponding issue of credit.

The essential difference from the old system is that there the bankers made the entries — creating bank-credit which was loaned to the government and also to the people at interest.

In this new system, the United States government would write its own notes which, upon being passed out to its citizens in exchange for goods and services, would become their medium of exchange.

The question may arise as to whether it is proper for the government to borrow this way, to give its note, to be used as money. Of course, it is. All our money has been notes for many years. Further, any of us may give his note in payment for goods or services and, if there is confidence that the note will be paid, it may be passed as cash from one person to another in trade. The Constitution, Article I, Section 8, provides that Congress borrow on the credit of the United States and then pay the debts: what better way than this? The government notes shall be a promise to pay by accepting them for taxes, which, in the last analysis, is the only way any government can pay its debts.

Congress not only has the power to create money; that is its duty. Further, as Lincoln said, it is the government's greatest opportunity to create a better life for its citizens.

Creation of Bank-Credit for Use of the Federal Government

The creation of bank-credit for use by the Federal government is based upon the following principal:

The United States Treasury Department of Money is owned by all the people and, as the ledger entries here (creating this bank-credit) is an indebtedness of all the people, it follows that bank-credit used for all the people (for their United States government expenses) shall bear no interest.

Remember that there is no reason why the government should pay interest on these notes, as would be the case if creditors were obliged to wait for some distant due date for payment, for the notes themselves are money, and may be used as cash in making purchases, paying bills, or as a storehouse of wealth the moment they are received.

Following this principal the United States Treasury Banks, under Congressional control, shall create, by entry upon their books and computers, bank-credit to meet every United States Government expense. This bank-credit is moved out to the various U.S. Government departments by furnishing these departments with slips of deposit and a properly printed supply of blank checks.

Creation of United States Treasury Bank-Credit for Loan

When the United States Treasury Banks (owned by all the people) lend money for use by only a part of the people, these loans shall be secured, shall bear interest, and shall be returned and canceled upon the same ledgers or computers upon which they were created. The interest paid on these loans shall accure to the profits of all the people in reducing taxes. Following these principals, the loan of United States Bank-Credit shall be done in three ways:

I. States, Counties and Cities

    Loaned to State, County and City Governments, for Congress-approved needs, after the citizens of these local governments have voted to secure these loans with interest-bearing bonds payable to the United States Treasury Banks. The interest here would be low, allowing progress without the deadening weight of excessive interest. This is the only money these divisions of government should be allowed to borrow.

II. To Commercial Banks

    Loaned to commercial banks at interest for reloan to their customers at an advance in interest. This differential in interest shall be sufficient to pay bankers for good, efficient services and no more. Money is too close to the heart of our economy to allow anyone an excess profit on it.

This bank-credit, created only by the United States Treasury Banks shall be reloaned by the commercial banks dollar for dollar (no discounting). This shall be the only bank-credit (money) the commercial banks may lend. They shall not lend either their own or their customers' money and Fractional Reserve Banking should be absolutely forbidden.

When the bank credit now on loan by commercial banks is repaid and extinguished, the amount of money will be greatly reduced, and the value of the dollar would be much higher — perhaps ten times as high. Debts and prices should be correspondingly reduced. From then on the amount of money should be, and could be carefully controlled enough, but never more than enough.

III. Building and Loan Associations

Man, deprived of his home, and, as a renter, forced into a crowded government apartment, perhaps with uncongenial or criminal neighbors, has already lost much of the meaning of life. Like all animals, man, by instinct, craves an area of earth he can call his own — a home.

The answer to housing is a dedicated system of Building and Loan Associations which would help worthy, reliable, industrious people finance their homes without the crushing interest rates of the present.

The United States Treasury banks shall, at the discretion of Congress, create and lend, at low interest, bank-credit to all accredited Building and Loan Associations to be loaned by them at an approved higher interest rate. Here, too, this is the only money these associations should be allowed to lend.

These institutions shall be required to limit their activities to the function their name implies.

Forms of Money

So far we have spoken of bank-credit money. This is the real money of the nation. Most money remains in this form. Hundreds of billions of dollars of bank-credit money are created by entries on ledgers or computers; are transferred by deposit slips and by checks returned for cancelation on the same books or computers which created them.

Currency

The word "currency" is defined in the *Century Dictionary* as the most rapid part of a stream and also as money that passes from hand to hand.

The currency of the new system shall be coins, as at present, and the printed government notes. These notes shall be of denominations $1, $5, $10, $20, $50, and $100, and shall bear the name:

"UNITED STATES NOTE"

and a distinguishing mark of the new system. These shall be our only legal tender note.

To put currency in its proper perspective, it might be well to bear in mind that this pocket money is for use in small transactions only, to avoid bookkeeping on petty amounts.

The United States Notes and the coins have their claims for value printed or stamped upon them, thus plainly showing on their face the amount of indebtedness the United States government owes the bearer. If a man has three one-dollar bills in his pocket it is evident that the government owes him three dollars in tax credits.

Supplying Currency

It shall be the duty of the United States Treasury banks to supply currency upon request and in exchange for Commercial bank checks to meet the requirements of these banks.

In explanation, the Commercial banks can borrow from the United States Treasury banks, and pay interest upon, either bank credit or currency.

Notes of Old System Recalled

The United States Treasury banks shall, from time to time, place in each commercial bank an amount of United

States notes, sufficient to exchange for notes of the former system, as fast as these come into the bank.

The old notes shall be sent to the United States Treasury banks to be credited against the new ones and then shredded.

Clearing Checks

The United States Treasury banks shall clear checks as at present. The actual expenses of these operations shall be borne by the commercial bank's customers accommodated.

Rationale of These Provisions

To leave the banker's foot in the door would allow their super lawyers and other agents to contrive every kind of trickery and evasion and eventually nullify any reform.

Any monetary reform must be definite, effective, easily understood and complete. It should be, as near as possible, foolproof against evasion and fraud.

Only in this way can the governors of the United States Treasury Department of Money have the information to control money; the power to supply money when and where needed; to withhold money when there is too much in circulation, and to calculate the tax required to keep the system in balance.

Money must flow continually through the economy. It should not be allowed to stagnate in pools aside from the main stream. Nothing must be allowed to obstruct its free flow outward to the people, on through the economy, and return to be canceled at its source.

The commercial banks shall pay no interest on money deposited by its customers. They shall make a charge for the money's safety and for the convenience of a checking account.

142

Commercial banks shall not lend their customers' money nor lend their own money. To allow them to do so would defeat the purpose of this reform. It is proposed here that the government furnish all money for loans, and receive all interest (above cost of handling), and with this interest cancel many of the notes (money) it issues for government expenses. This would allow the government to greatly reduce taxes — a relief to all its citizens — their just right from their ownership of money.

These restrictions on private banking lie at the very heart of any monetary reform worthy of the name. Straddling the fence here has caused the confusion so evident in all earlier attempts to devise a workable monetary reform.

Some bankers will elect to close rather than go along with a system which has no rake-off for them. Congress could buy these banks and lease them to the employers who had been running them for the overlords.

An honest government could run our own banks.

North Dakota has its own state bank, founded in 1919, with capital of $2 million. It saved thousands of North Dakota farmers in the Great Depression, and has been the source of that state's financial strength. The bank handles state funds and has over 5,000 depositors.

A postcard from North Dakota's Deputy Treasurer, Robert E. Hanson, November 29, 1976, states:

"North Dakota does not have any debt. In fact, it will have a surplus of from $170-$185 million at the end of 1977 fiscal year (June 30, 1977)."

North Dakota is lowering taxes.

Singapore:
This System in Operation

Martin A. Larson, writing in *The Spotlight*, November 29, 1982, states:

"When I visited Singapore in 1981, I conferred with a number of knowledgeable local individuals concerning their economy in order to understand Singapore's economic miracle. I concluded that it had become possible because the government there is responsible for fiscal policies; that there is no fractional reserve banking; that all currency is issued by the government — the funds draw the maximum rate of interest — within 15 years a modern civilization has been created. Since deficit spending is prohibited, there is no government debt.

"Almost everyone has modern housing, and those who retire enjoy generous pensions without any cost to the younger and producing generation.

"Furthermore, there is almost no public welfare."[3]

Schematic Diagram of
PROPOSED MONETARY SYSTEM
(Nothing but Bookkeeping)

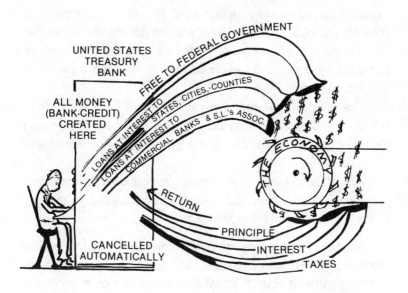

To show —

Continuous flow of money from its source; its passage through the economy and its continuous cancelation on the same computer.

The upper horn of issue represents the creation of money to pay all government expenses. As this money is for the use of all our people — those who own the system — it bears no interest. The other horns of issue represent the creation and loan of money to that part of our people who must borrow from the whole. The principal of all loans must be secured, and returned to balance and cancel their issue. Interest charges on these loans are payable to the Treasury Banks for the benefit of all our people, borrower and non-borrower alike.

The return of the issued money is shown in the lower horns. The upper one of these represents payments of principal of money. This is on the way to cancelation. The middle return horn represents the continuous return, for cancelation of money being paid to the government as interest on loans. This interest will go far toward canceling the outgo for government expenses. Any deficit will be canceled by a carefully planned tax levy — represented by the lower horn.

The only federal government debts will be current ones, for the notes being continually issued are being continually paid — that is, they are being continually collected and canceled.

All of this incoming money from principal, interest, sales and taxes is canceled — totally obliterated — making room for continuing outpouring.

Money, the peoples' money, their standard of value and medium of exchange issued, as described here, forever pouring from its source, must flow through our economy in a never ending stream like water flowing over millions of millwheels. It must then be collected and canceled, so that the outflow can continue. To allow a few privileged individuals to set a price on every drop, to dam it up for private profit, is to eventually bring the entire system to a halt.

CHECK OFF INTEREST
AS A PRIVATE PRIVILEGE
INTEREST IS OBSOLETE

Under the proposed plan, the interest you might pay would be paid on your own money, used for your own benefit, and obliterated. It could never be hoarded or used by financiers to manipu-

146

late the economy, or to cause inflation by presenting enormous claims for unearned wealth.

A full account with details of the proposed monetary system is given in ''A Bill for Congress'' at the end of this book.

Balancing the Books

Balancing the United States Treasury Banks' ledgers and computers and, incidentally, the Federal budget, is as simple as the rest of the system. It should be mandatory.

The books of those departments creating and lending money at interest are in exact balance at all times, for there are, on deposit in these departments, bonds or other evidence of debt for every loan that has been made. As the principals of these loans are paid, the principals, along with notations and securities of their issue, are canceled.

The interest from these loans does not affect the balance in these divisions, for as fast as it is collected it is passed on to the department supplying the government — to help cancel the issue there. Our only concern then is to maintain a constant near balance of the books of the department, issuing money for federal government expenses. This is now discussed and provided for.

Debit

The money for all government expenses is created for the expense of the printing. The amount issued should be adequate, but no more. A stop must be put to the idea that the treasury is a bottomless pocket of money from which officials and citizens can continually strive for higher salaries, pensions, and expense accounts; make unneeded jobs for kinsmen and friends; and hand out to those who have befriended them.

Notwithstanding all this, the Department of the United States Treasury banks charged with creating and furnishing money for government expenses would be almost constantly issuing bank credit by entries on their books or computers.

Credit (Income)

Such entries should be constantly canceled by an inflowing of funds from three sources: interest; taxes adjusted to the need; and sales of natural resources, government property, and royalties.

1. Interest

   This interest is from other divisions of the United States Treasury banks which receive it from loans to state and local governments; commercial banks and building and loan associations. The rates of interest should be low, but would be, in the aggregate, a very great amount.

2. Taxes

   The only taxes that will be necessary after monetary reform will be just such tariffs and sales taxes as are necessary, after interest and royalty incomes mentioned above, to maintain the legitimate functions of the federal government under the *Constitution.* Since most current bureaucracies are engaging in regulatory functions never permitted by the *Constitution,* they should be dismantled. Article Ten of the Bill of Rights says, ''The powers not delegated to the United States by the Constitution, nor prohibited by it to the states, are reserved to the states respectively, or to the people.''

148

3. Lease of Natural Resources on Government Lands

The federal government now owns roughly one-third of all United States land. Here and there through much of this land, there are enormous deposits of coal, oil, gas, shale and uranium. With the exception of parks and land which should be preserved for posterity, these natural resources should be leased to large companies capable of developing them. The lease should not be, as now, for very little, recovered by the company in higher charges, but for half or more of the final value. Money from these leases, flowing in year after year, will help in the reduction of taxes.

Congressional investigations and legislation must assure that no part of the international banking community or multinational conglomerate industry be allowed to purchase these lands. If this ''invisible government'' which has so long pauperized our land and our people were allowed to settle its bad debts with our national, natural resources, America would be doomed.

Defaulting Foreign Loans

It must never be forgotten that the enormous debts caused by foreign aid and trade are the direct result of Wall Street pressure on Congress to shift private bank debt onto the backs of the American taxpayer. No provision of the *Constitution* gives the bankers the right to demand this, or Congress the right to do it. In the final analysis, the debts of the international banks, unwisely made and without hope of repayment, are their own concern.

Therefore, if any sale of resources must be urged to settle the bankers' debt, it should be that of their own resources.

149

". . . But we finally accomplished it and gave to the people of this Republic the greatest blessing they ever had — their own paper to pay their own debts" (Abraham Lincoln).

CHAPTER 14

Light at the End
of a Long, Dark Tunnel

If the reforms advocated in this book are followed, those who have bled our American economy for many decades will be removed and the Republic can be saved. Here are some of the benefits which will result:

- Cancelation at once of some $130 billion of United States bonds now held in vaults of the Federal Reserve — thus saving the tax we pay for their interest.

- Never again would there be an additional issue of United States bonds.

- The Federal Budget would always be in near balance.

- A stable dollar. Never again either inflation or deflation.

- No more recessions or depressions.

- Low taxes. Interest paid to the government would greatly reduce taxes. This benefit would extend to

151

the interest payer.

- Low interest. Interest rates would not be at the mercy of the bankers. They would be set by Congress, commensurate with the needs of the nation.

- Interest, once paid, would not be piled up by bankers to further enslave the nation, but would be canceled and the money paying them return to nothingness. Interest would be a blessing instead of a curse.

- Break the stranglehold of the bankers and prevent the further takeover of the nation.

- End of usury. Those eligible to borrow money could do so without the deadening charges of today.

- Money furnished to states, counties, and cities at low interest, allowing for rapid progress. The low interest rate would allow a reduction in taxes.

Federal taxes would be used only to maintain a balanced budget. Once a return to true, Constitutional government is effected, the federal government will be so much smaller and its functions so reduced that this will not be difficult.

Interest paid to the government for loans of money and savings through an end of the total welfare state would be the primary ways financial stability will be restored. Those formerly destitute who desire to work should find many opportunities in the proliferation of small businesses which will spring out of such an improved economic climate.

As huge bureaucracies are shut down for good, there will be great savings from the cost of their operations, including salaries. Of course, those formerly bureaucrats will have to adjust to joining the producing sector of the economy. They will have to ''find a need and fill it.'' Out of this will come a genuine increase in the gross national product. Instead of a parasitic drain on the economy, there will again be genuine additions to it.

After monetary reform, the income tax should not be needed. Then each taxpayer will keep much of his earnings instead of having it taken from him by taxes on income or wages.

Repeal of inheritance taxes, started in the Reagan Administration, is another vital area of economic reform. Anyone should be able to pass on to his family his home or farm, his savings, or even a moderately large fortune. Such continuity of wealth is the very basis for economic family stability. It allows each successive generation to begin life from an advanced position, to build on what has gone before, rather than from nothing, as most families do at present.

The welfare of each individual citizen should be our aim. The harboring of illegal aliens who take American jobs and welfare benefits can no longer be tolerated. At this writing, ''there are more officers guarding the grounds of the U.S. Capitol than there are patrolling all the borders of the entire United States.''[2]

The government and entire economy cannot be geared to the task of furnishing an ''incentive'' and a guaranteed profit for those who, having gathered in most of the wealth, want the rest of it. Daily advancing their claims against every citizen of the nation, the collusion between Big Business, Big Government, and Big Banking has nearly destroyed this Constitutional republic.

Under the new system, genuine free enterprise would have a chance to survive. Then welfare benefits to the helpless would be a privilege, an overflow from a productive economy, instead of a burden. The Old Testament provided for the poor by allowing them to glean the fields after the owners had reaped the harvest. Thus, the poor were granted the dignity of work to provide their bread, as well as the mercy of gifts from the property and productivity of others.

The monetary reforms urged in this book will help to bring to an end the stranglehold which international bankers and the multinational conglomerates they own have placed on America and the whole world. Such books as Pat Brooks' *The Return of the Puritans* and Des Griffin's *Fourth Reich of the Rich* show how the super-rich have promoted both corporate fascism and world socialism at the same time. They go beyond the scope of this book, and are recommended for further study. My next book, *Honest Government,* will deal with reforms needed to bring the United States back under the *Constitution,* as this money monopoly over the nation is finally broken.

In Conclusion

This book has not dealt with idle, intellectual concerns. We are facing either the life or death of this republic. A nation's monetary system is to its economy what blood is to the human body, and ours is being bled dry.

As a surgeon, I stayed with my patients during their time of crisis. Patriots must unite, elect, and stand behind officials who will see monetary reform through to its completion. Eternal vigilance is still the price of freedom.

It is folly to imagine that the financiers who have controlled our beloved land for so long — and indeed, the whole world — will give it up without a struggle. Ours is not a rocking chair age, but one in which the very foundations of civilization will be shaken. The hurricane of convulsive change is already upon us.

"It is the business of the future to be dangerous — the major advances in civilization are processes that all but wreck the societies in which they occur"

(Alfred North Whitehead, *Adventures in Ideas*).

It may seem that we are hoping for too much; that it is impossible to overthrow this giant combine and recover our government and our monetary system. But there is a way.

Those leaders who are rallying the voters can call for a return to Almighty God and His righteousness, and seek His help.

His conditions for blessing are very clearly given in II Chronicles 7:14: "If my people, which are called by my name, shall humble themselves, and pray, and seek my face, and turn from their wicked ways; then will I hear from heaven, and will forgive their sin, and will heal their land."

As reform comes, the greatest care must be taken to prevent traitors, in the pay of financiers, from worming their way into the control of the reform and delivering it into their masters' hands. We cannot trust lobbyists or public officials, intent only on saving their own jobs. Only patriots with the willingness to lay down "their lives, their fortunes, their sacred honor," can be trusted with this work.

Contemporary "Sons of Liberty" will be as careful with their wording of the new monetary bill as were the Founding Fathers with that of the *Constitution*. One phrase — indeed, one word slipped in, or used inadvertently — may nullify the whole movement.

My own thirty years of research which have led to the writing of these two books have culminated in the suggested Bill for Monetary Reform in the Appendix. It is my fervent hope that it will receive serious consideration by the patriots who must reclaim our freedoms, under our *Constitution*.

To you, who are among their number, I leave the torch.

Appendix

A MONETARY BILL
FOR CONGRESS

A Bill

To vest in Congress of the United States of America the sole, absolute and unconditional power and duty to issue the nation's money and to regulate the value thereof, pursuant to ARTICLE I, Sec. 8 (5) of the CONSTITUTION OF THE UNITED STATES OF AMERICA, BE IT ENACTED BY THE SENATE AND HOUSE OF REPRESENTATIVES OF THE UNITED STATES OF AMERICA IN CONGRESS ASSEMBLED, THAT

(a) Pursuant to Section 30 of THE FEDERAL RESERVE ACT OF DECEMBER 23, 1913, the Federal Reserve Act of 1913 and all amendments and laws dealing with it and with banking and/or in any way conflicting with this new law are hereby repealed.

(b) In compliance with the methods for liquidation as laid down in the Federal Reserve Act of December 23, 1913, the Secretary of the Treasury is directed to pay the Federal Reserve Member Banks, a matching amount paid by them, for their stock. Following this the Secretary of the Treasury shall take possession of the stock and the Federal

159

Reserve in the name of the United States of America.

There is hereby authorized the appropriation, from any available fund, an amount of money, as may be necessary to carry out all provisions of this bill.

(c) The outgoing Federal Reserve officials are hereby directed and required to surrender to the Secretary of the Treasury, acting for Congress, keys and possession of all property of every nature, now held under the Federal Reserve Act of 1913, and its amendments, together with its record in their usual and present condition.

(d) The name of this organization shall be changed to "The United States Treasury Department of Money," and the names of the 12 District Banks changed to the "United States Treasury Banks" of their respective cities. Headquarters of the system shall be located at its building in the nation's capital.

(e) The governing body of the system shall consist of three governors, a chairman and two members, appointed by the President with advice and approval of Congress. The term of office of the first appointee shall be two years; the second, four years; and the third, six years. All later appointments shall be for a period of six years. None of these shall be reappointed more than once. Any official of the bank may be removed by a majority vote of no confidence by the lower house of Congress. These three governors, under the Secretary of the Treasury and finally under control of Congress, shall be charged with formulating rules, and with efficient and honest operation of the system. Their conferences with lobbyists and other self-seekers shall be recorded and open for public inspection. Any acceptance of favors or remuneration direct or indirect from any lobbyist (used in its broadest meaning) shall be grounds for dismissal. The system shall be manned with competent, dedicated, civil service employees. Any of the former system's clerical and/or service force who wish to continue, can qualify, and will pledge allegiance to the new department shall be retained.

(f) All United States bonds in vault of Federal Reserve, taken over with the old system, shall be tabulated and shredded. There shall never again be an additional issue of United States bonds.

(g) The United States Treasury Department of money shall forthwith resume the function of issuing, supplying and controlling the nation's money.

Each issue shall consist of an entry of bank credit upon ledgers or computers of United States District Banks. (This signifies a note of indebtedness of all people in the nation.)

This bank credit shall be materialized in two ways:

(1) By deposit slips showing the amount, in dollars, credited to the checking account of each recipient.

(2) By standardized tokens called currency:

United States notes of 1, 5, 10, 20, 50 and 100 dollar denominations. These notes shall bear distinguishing marks of the new system. They shall replace all notes of the old system as those come into commercial banks.

Coins: minted as at present.

This money shall be the only United States money. It shall be full legal tender; receivable for all debts, public and private.

It shall be passed into circulation by supplying it without interest to: The United States Government.

By lending at interest to: State, County and City Governments, Commercial Banks, Building and Loan Associations.

161

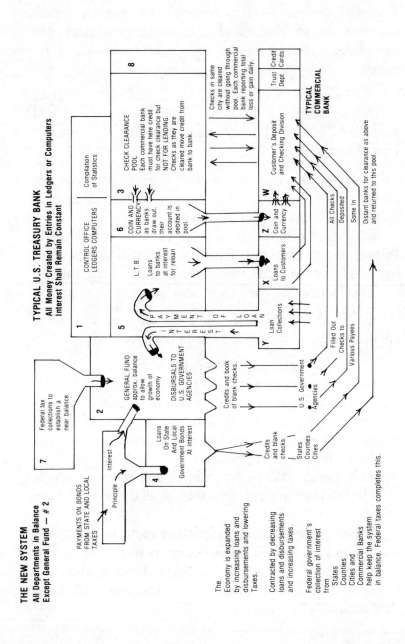

THE NEW SYSTEM
All Departments in Balance
Except General Fund — # 2

TYPICAL U.S. TREASURY BANK
All Money Created by Entries in Ledgers or Computers
Interest Shall Remain Constant

PAYMENTS ON BONDS
FROM STATE AND LOCAL
TAXES

7 — Federal tax collections to establish a near balance.

CONTROL OFFICE
LEDGERS COMPUTERS

Compilation of Statistics

8

1

Principle   Interest

2 — GENERAL FUND approx. balance to allow growth of economy

DISBURSALS TO U.S. GOVERNMENT AGENCIES

Credits and book of blank checks.

4 — Loans On State And Local Government Bonds At Interest

Credits and blank checks.
States
Counties
Cities

5 — PAYMENT OF INTEREST OF LOAN

L.T.B. Loans to banks at interest for reloan

6 — COIN AND CURRENCY as banks draw out. their account is debited in pool.

3 — CHECK CLEARANCE POOL
Each commercial bank must have here credit for check clearance but NOT FOR LENDING. Checks as they are cleared move credit from bank to bank.

Loan Collections

X — Loans to Customers

Z — Coin and Currency

W — Customer's Deposit and Checking Division

Y — U.S. Government Agencies

Filled Out Checks to Various Payees

All Checks Deposited

Some In

Distant banks for clearance as above and returned to this pool.

Checks in same city are cleared without going through pool. Each commercial bank reporting total loss or gain daily.

Trust Dept.   Credit Cards

TYPICAL COMMERCIAL BANK

The Economy is expanded by increasing loans and disbursements and lowering Taxes.

Contracted by decreasing loans and disbursements and increasing taxes.

Federal government's collection of interest from
States
Counties
Cities and
Commercial Banks
help keep the system in balance. Federal taxes completes this.

OPERATION OF THE UNITED STATES TREASURY DEPARTMENT OF MONEY

(h) Headquarters of the Department shall house the officers of the Governors and their staff, and shall be at the Capital of the United States. This shall be the nerve center of the System. Its offices and its battery of computers shall be connected to each District Bank. Reports from District Banks shall be stored here and shall at all times be open to any member of Congress.

A schematic diagram is given to illustrate a typical United States Treasury Bank and a typical Commercial Bank and to show their interrelationship.

In this diagram the Chief departments of the United States Treasury bank are designated by numbers as follows:

No. 1: Main office.

No. 2: General fund — supply the U.S. Government.

No. 3: Check Clearance Pool.

No. 4: Loans to State, City and County Governments.

No. 5: Loans to Commercial Banks and Building and Loan Associations.

No. 6: Coin and Currency departments.

No. 7: Federal tax receiving department.

No. 8: Foreign Trade and Exchange.

The Chief Departments of the Commercial Bank are represented by Capital letters as follows:

"W": Customers and Checking Divisions.

"X": Loans to Customers.

"Y": Loan Collections.

"Z": Coin and Currency.

CENTRAL OFFICE OF REGIONAL BANK

The officials in the central office of the United States Regional Bank, shown on the diagram as No. 1, upon receiving an order from the bank governor's office at the Capital, shall transmit it to the proper division of their own bank, and bear final responsibility for its proper execution. They shall also direct the accounting, the statistical gathering, the analyzing of data from their section of the economy and transmit all reports to the main U.S. Treasury Monetary System's headquarters at the Capital, as part of the material to be considered in governing the system.

METHOD OF SUPPLYING MONEY TO THE UNITED STATES GOVERNMENT

Each week the Secretary of the Treasury shall prepare, for Monday of the coming week, a list of United States Monetary requirements, as appropriated by Congress, and shall submit this list to the governors of the United States Treasury Department of Money. These officials shall send the request to the Central Office (1) of the District Bank which is to be charged with supplying the money.

The Central Office (No. 1 on the diagram) shall order its Department for Disbursements to the United States Government (No. 2 on the diagram), to create the money by setting up upon its ledgers or computers bank-credit for the United States Government's Department or Agency designated.

A deposit slip for this amount, together with a supply of United Treasury District Bank checks carrying a subhead of the department accommodated, is sent to that department.

These checks, when written by the proper officials, paid out and properly endorsed, shall be accepted at the Customer's Section (W on the diagram) of any commercial bank. Should the bearer cash the check, the money immediately goes into circulation. Should he deposit the check, he would receive a passbook and increase his checking account.

In either case the check shall be sent to the region's United States Treasury Bank Check Clearance Pool (Department No. 3). The Commercial Bank's credit in the pool is raised by that amount and the check is forwarded in the U.S. Treasury Bank's Department (2) of Issue. The check we have been following is there stamped ''Paid.'' The government department for which the money was created is debited to the amount of the check and the check returned to its writer.

The entries on books or computers of Department 2, as on all books where money is created, remain as liabilities of the United States until canceled by collections, in this instance, from interest and taxes.

LOANS TO STATE AND LOCAL GOVERNMENTS

In like manner, the United States Treasury Banks shall, for Congress Approved Social Needs, upon orders received at the Main Office (No. 1), provide requested loans to State, City and County governments.

Guidelines for terms and interest shall be laid down by Congress. They should be lenient enough to allow rapid progress without overwhelming local taxation.

The Division of the United States Treasury Bank charged with this duty (No. 4) creates the money by entries in their ledgers or computers. A deposit slip and a supply of blank checks with proper subheads are exchanged for duly executed, interest-bearing bonds.

These checks when properly filled out and endorsed, are receivable at any Commercial Bank (Dept. W) from which they are sent through clearing pool (3) of the United States

Treasury Bank and on to Department 4, where, after being stamped paid, they are returned to the writer.

The bonds are retained as security for the debt.

Payment of these bonds shall be made at Department 4, by separate checks, one for principal and one for interest, drawn on the local or state government's account in some Commercial bank. The amount of check for principal is noted on the bond and is then subtracted from the ledger's original entry, canceling that issue of money. The check for interest is sent to the General Fund, Division No. 2, where it is credited on United States Government's disbursements canceling that amount.

The checks are routed to Check Clearance Pool No. 3, reducing the Commercial Bank's balance, and on through that bank to the minor government official who wrote the check.

PRIVATELY OWNED FINANCIAL INSTITUTIONS

The true personal ownership (not nominees) of all privately owned financial institutions shall be recorded by officers of such institutions with the U.S. Treasury Department, and also in the office in which the institution does business, and shall during business hours be open to the general public.

COMMERCIAL BANKS

All commercial banks shall be under the direct supervision and control of the Secretary of the Treasury, acting for Congress, who shall have them examined at irregular intervals by rotated Civil Service bank examiners and accountants. These officials shall be charged with reporting any irregularity or failure to follow laws enacted by Congress.

It shall be the duty of the United States District Banks to create and lend money to all Commercial Banks, for reloan, dollar for dollar, to the Commercial Bank's customers.

To implement this provision each United States Treasury Bank shall use its "Loans to Banks" (Division No. 5 on the Diagram).

Upon order from its Central Office (No. 1) this division shall set up upon its ledgers a Loans to Banks right for each Commercial Bank in its district (by this is meant the right to ask that money be created for them to relend). This operation shall, hereinafter, be referred to as a Drawing Right (DR). There shall be no reserve required, and no interest charged until the Commercial Bank check drawn against it is dated. The Drawing Right is evidenced by an authorization from the U.S. Treasury Bank of the district.

The amount of this account will vary from time to time in accordance with the prevailing Congressional policy as to expansion or contraction of the economy, and also as to the approved needs of the bank.

The money so supplied shall be the only money either borrowed or loaned by Commercial Banks. There shall be no loan of the bank's own money or of their customer's money. Fractional Reserve Banking — the private creation of bank credit money — is forbidden.

LOAN DEPARTMENTS
OF THE COMMERCIAL BANKS

It is hereby ordered and required that each Commercial Bank establish a loan department (X on the diagram) having the sole function of borrowing money from the United States Treasury Banks and lending that same day, dollar for dollar, to their customers. This loan division shall contain no vault, no money, no claims for money. Its equipment shall be its furniture, records, ledgers, and computers, and its stock in trade shall be its Loans to Banks and its blank United States Treasury District Bank checks carrying a subhead of the Commercial Bank.

METHOD OF MAKING LOANS
AT COMMERCIAL BANKS

In making a loan the Commercial Bank's lending officer shall, after making all records of the loan and receiving the customer's note, fill out a Drawing Right check for the full amount (no discount) and giving this check to the borrower, instruct him to present it to the Customer's Division (W) of that same bank. There he is given a deposit slip and a book of blank checks. When the Drawing Right Check is received at the Check Clearance Pool (No. 3), the Commercial Bank's account is raised to that amount. From there the check is forwarded to the Rights Division (No. 5 on the Diagram) which creates the money by an entry in their ledger. This is a debit to the Commercial Bank's D.R.

The check, stamped paid, is retained as evidence of the transaction (a note against the commercial bank) until the money with interest is returned.

PAYMENT OF COMMERCIAL BANK LOAN

At the due date, unless there is a renewal, the bank's customer shall pay the note and interest at the bank's collection department (Y on the diagram).

RETURN OF LTB LOANS BY COMMERCIAL BANKS

Upon customer's payment of a note the Commercial Bank shall pay, in separate checks, its principal and the

168

government's share of the interest.

The check for the principal, arriving at Loans to Banks Division (No. 5) cancels its loan, and raises the Commercial Bank's drawing right. The check for interest is forwarded to the General Fund (No. 2), where it cancels, to that amount, money which has been spent in running the government. Both checks are cleared in Department 3, marked paid, and returned to the Commercial Bank.

(The money, both principal and interest, created by entries on computers, has served its purpose, and is, on computers, totally obliterated — making way for a fresh outpouring.)

The differential between the rate of interest the United States Treasury Bank's charge for the D.R. loan and the interest the Commercial Bank charges its customer for this money shall be sufficient to pay for good service and no more.

METHOD OF SUPPLYING CURRENCY AND COIN

Department No. 6 of the United States Treasury Bank is charged with providing currency (U.S. Treasury notes and coins) to the Commercial Banks.

The Commercial Bank needing currency sends from its Department "Z" a request, accompanied by its Special Drawing Right Check to the United States Treasury Bank Department No. 6.

The Board of Governors shall make rules for payment of interest on this currency.

COMMERCIAL BANK DEPOSITS

The Commercial Banks shall receive their customer's deposits for which the bank shall make a service charge for providing security and for the convenience of a checking account. The banks shall not lend this money.

SUPPLYING MONEY TO BUILDING AND LOAN ASSOCIATIONS

All building and loan associations must meet the standards formulated by the governors of the United States Treasury Department of Money, and shall operate under their direction and control.

Building and Loan associations shall be granted Loans To Banks to supply the money they may lend. The methods of making these loans of collecting, of handling interest, and of reporting, shall be in all respects similar to those of Commercial banks. The differential of the two interest rates shall be their total income.

These associations are hereby forbidden to accept or keep deposits or currency from any source. Their accounts and checks shall be handled through commercial banks. Their sole function shall be financing of homes, apartments and other dwellings and their appurtenances.

COMMERCIAL BANK AND BUILDING AND LOAN ASSOCIATION LOANS OUTSTANDING AS OF THE DAY THE FEDERAL ACT IS REPEALED

As the money available for loans by these institutions must first be borrowed from the United States Treasury Banks, there will be, upon repeal of the Federal Reserve Act, many billions of dollars in Commercial Bank and Building and Loan Association — loans without foundation. These loans are hereby declared valid — debts owed by the debtors — to be immediately converted into loans of the new system.

MEETING DRAWING RIGHT REQUIREMENTS
FOR THESE EXISTING LOANS

All Commercial Banks and building and loan associations are directed and required immediately to furnish the United States Treasury Banks in their district full details of all outstanding loans. Following this they shall supply the proper foundations for these loans by calling in all borrowers, as fast as they can be accommodated, and convert the old loans into new ones, using the methods described above. The date of conversion shall be the date of signing this bill into law. After that date every such loan, already made or made later, shall be from matching dollar for dollar, interest bearing loans drawn from Special Rights Departments of United States Treasury Banks.

PRIVATE LOANS AND GRANTS FORBIDDEN

Except as already provided and except for welfare payments and grants for disaster areas, there shall be no advance of money or credit, no guarantee against loss from the United States Government to any individual or to any privately owned corporations.

UNIFORM INTEREST RATES

Interest rates, perhaps different for different types of loans, shall be set by Congress and shall be uniform throughout every financial institution under Congressional control, thus discouraging the shifting of funds from place to place.

INTEREST FROM GOVERNMENT LOANS

The interest collected by the United States Treasury Banks on every dollar loaned to states, counties, cities, commercial banks and to building and loan associations, while at a low rate, will, in the aggregate, withdraw large amounts of money from circulation. This cancelation, on the books, of the United States indebtedness will greatly lower the amount of Federal taxes which would otherwise be required to keep the system in balance.

The cancelation of all interest collected will not only tend to stabilize the dollar, but will allow more outpouring for worthy causes.

BALANCING THE BOOKS AND COMPUTERS

With one exception the accounts of all departments of the United States Treasury Banks shall be in balance at all times.

The exception is the General Fund (Department 2). Here, for United States government expenses, there is an almost continuous creation of bank credit by entries in its ledgers, and an outflow of this credit. Almost continually, too, is the inflow of bank credit from collected interest, canceling many of these entries. This cancelation is, at the same time, being continued by the inflow of bank credit from Federal taxes collected by Department No. 7.

This tax is to be adjusted by Congress to keep the General Fund Department No. 2 in approximate balance at all times.

CLEARING CHECKS

The United States Treasury Banks shall, in their Clearance Pool (No. 3), clear not only their own checks but all out-of-town checks for commercial banks. Also, at the close of each day's business they shall require and receive from the commercial banks in their district their aggregate loss or gain of checking accounts.

As checks are cleared and as reports from commercial banks are received, bank credit in Pool 3 shall be shifted to and from accounts of these commercial banks.

The service of clearing checks shall be charged to the receiving commercial banks which, in turn, pass the charge to their customers.

FOREIGN TRADE AND EXCHANGE

Following instructions from the United States Treasury Banks' central office No. 1, the bank's department No. 8 shall oversee and control all foreign trade and exchange of its district.

A buyer of foreign goods must send his request and a check on a commercial bank to that bank. His account is debited. The check is forwarded to the U.S.T. District Bank department No. 8 for exchange. The check is routed through Pool 3 where the commercial bank's credit is debited, to that amount and on to commercial bank to be returned to the writer.

Department No. 8, using its own bank credit, then completes the transaction in accordance with agreements or treaties of an international bank or the country involved. The process is reversed when a foreign sale is made.

The commercial bank is charged for the transaction, the fee then passed on to the customer obliged.

THE ISSUE AND CONTROL OF ITS MONEY
IS FUNDAMENTAL TO A FREE NATION

This system shall be kept totally independent and free from the control, interference and influence of each and every private financier, politician acting individually, all foreign governments and other organizations, as follows:

UNITED STATES MONETARY INSTITUTE

It shall be the duty of the House of Representatives Committee on Banking and Currency to furnish the Congress, for their consideration, complete plans for a United States Institute of Money, where career civil service officials can be trained in this new method of handling the finances of the nation, as well as foreign exchange and trade.

Congress shall have ultimate control over each and every financial institution dealing in its people's money; and shall, through the board of governors, lay down guidelines for the conducting of their business. To expedite and facilitate foreign trade and travel, the President may, with the advice of and subject to confirmation by Congress, enter into agreements with other governments as to methods of foreign exchange.

PENALTY FOR NON-COMPLIANCE

The board of governors may require any person engaged in any transaction referred to in this bill to furnish, under oath, complete information relative thereto, including the production of any books of account, contracts, letters or other papers, in connection therewith in the custody or control of such persons, either before or after such transactions are completed. The term ''person'' means an individual, partnership, association or corporation. Any individual, association, or any director, officer or employee thereof, violating any provisions of this Act shall be guilty of a misdemeanor and, upon conviction thereof, shall be fined $10,000.00, or if a natural person may, in addition to such fine, be imprisoned for a term not exceeding five years.

Upon conviction for a second offense, showing willful non-compliance and involving the authorized management of a financial institution to the penalty already set forth shall be added that of cancelation of the institution's charter.

Notes

The material for this book has, over the years, been drawn from so many sources that it is impossible to know or name all of them. An earnest attempt has been made to give credit for direct borrowed material. Many credits and references are given in the text. Others are listed below.

I am very grateful to the publishers and authors who have so kindly given permission to use copyrighted material.

Many quotations have been used, not only because they express their points so well, but because I want you to read the exact words of these gifted and authoritative writers.

PREFACE

U.S. News & World Report, October 12, 1981.

CHAPTER 2

[1]Herbert Cescinsky, *English Furniture,* 1937, Garden City Publishing Company, Garden City, N.Y., page 5.

[2]Claude H. Van Tyne, *The Causes of the War of Independence,* 1922, Houghton, Mifflin Co., Boston & New York, Vol. 1, pages 3, 10, 12.

[3]Alexander Del Mar, *A History of Money in America,* 1966, Omni Publications, Hawthorne, California, page 75.

[4]*Ibid.,* page 77.

[5]*Ibid.,* page 79.

[6]Oliver Cushing Dwinell, *The Story of Our Money,* 1946, Forham Publishing Company, now handled by Omni Publications, Hawthorne, California, pages 23-28.

[7]Del Mar, op. cit., page 81.

[8]Del Mar, op. cit., page 83.

[9]*The Works of Benjamin Franklin,* Federal Edition, compiled and edited by John Biglow. Published and copyrighted by G.P. Putnams' Sons Publishing Company. Read *The Story of Our Money,* Omni Publications, Hawthorne, California, page 39.

[10]John R. Elsom: *Lightning Over the Treasury Building,* Seventh Printing, 1961. Forham Publishing Company, now Omni Publications, Hawthorne, California, page 30. Quotes from *Senate Document #23,* page 98, by Robert L. Owen, former Chairman, Committee on Banking and Currency, United States Senate.

[11]Del Mar, op. cit., page 96.

[12]Dwinell, op. cit., pages 46-53.

[13]Del Mar, op. cit., pages 96-116.

[14]*History of All Nations,* Vol. XXII, John Fiske, Independence of the New World, 1905. Lee Brothers and Company, Philadelphia and New York, pages 251-253. *A Primer on Money,* U.S. Government Printing Office, Wright Patman, 1964, page 15. *The History of Money in America,* Alexander Del Mar, Omni Publications, Hawthorne, California, pages 104, 114 and 115.

[15]*World Book Encyclopedia.*

[16]Fiske, op. cit., pages 301-302.

[17]Del Mar, op. cit., page 109.

[18]*The Writings of Thomas Jefferson,* Memorial Edition, Vol. X; published 1903, page 306.

[19]Dwinell, op. cit., page 84.

CHAPTER 3

[1]Jack C. Estrin, *American History Made Simple,* copyright © 1956, by Doubleday & Co., Inc. Reprinted by permission of publisher, page 98.

[2]Robert Friedberg, *Paper Money of the United States,* 6th edition, 1968. Coin & Currency Institute, Inc., New York, pages 10, 28-31.

[3]Oliver Cushing Dwinell, *The Story of Our Money,* page 115, quotes this from Emil Ludwig's *Lincoln,* translated by Eden and Cedar Paul, 1930; Boston; Little, Brown and Company.

[4]G.G. McGreer, *The Conquest of Poverty,* Second Edition, 1967, Omni Publications, page 169.

[5]Porter and Coats, *History of the Civil War in America,* Vol. III, 1883, Comte de Paris, page 413.

[6]Friedberg, op. cit., inscription on photographs of the notes.

[7]*A Primer on Money,* Committee on Banking and Currency, House of Representatives, 88th Congress, 2nd Session, August 5, 1964. Government Printing Office, Washington, C.C., page 48.

[8]McGreer, op. cit., page 205.

[9]Dwinell, op. cit., page 121. This book takes quotation from Carl Sandburg, *Abraham Lincoln, the War Years,* Harcourt, Brace, Jovanovich, Inc., New York, page 171. *Ibid.,* this book also has the statement about the sale of bonds, $1 for $1. Note.

[10]Congressional Record, House, July 17, 1969. H6023.

[11]McGreer, op. cit., pages 201-202.

[12]Alexander Del Mar, *A History of Monetary Crimes,* 1899, Cleaners Press, Washington, pages 73-82.

CHAPTER 4

[1]Within memory of author.

[2]Congressman Wright Patman, *A Primer on Money,* U.S. Government Printing Office, Washington, 1964, pages 56-57.

[3]*Ibid.,* page 54.

[4]H.S. Keenan, *The Federal Reserve Banks,* Noontide Press, Los Angeles, California, 1968 edition.

CHAPTER 5

[1]*The Federal Reserve Act of 1913 With Amendments and Laws Related to Banking,* 1966. Washington Government Printing Office.

[2]Sheldon Emry, *Billions for the Bankers and Debts for the People,* Christian Research, Inc., Minneapolis, Minnesota, page 2.

CHAPTER 6

[1]Wright Patman, *A Primer on Money,* August 5, 1964, and *Money Facts,* September 21, 1964, both published by U.S. Government Printing Office, Washington, D.C. Federal Reserve Act, as amended through 1971, compiled

under the direction of the Board of Governors of the Federal Reserve System in its Legal Division.

[2]Wright Patman, *A Primer on Money,* page 34.

[3]G.G. McGreer, *The Conquest of Poverty,* Second Edition, Omni Publications, Hawthorne, California, page 174.

[4]Wright Patman, *A Primer on Money,* page 38.

[5]Courtesy of Mark Andrews, Cape Coral, Florida.

CHAPTER 8

[1]Thomas Porter, *The Green Magicians,* Omni Publications, Hawthorne, California.

[2]*The Spotlight,* 300 Independence Avenue, Washington, D.C. 20003.

[3]*Newsweek,* Inc., January 12, 1970.

CHAPTER 9

[1]*The Miami Herald,* February 13, 1973.

[2]*The Spotlight,* 300 Independence Avenue, S.E., Washington, D.C. 20003, December 8, 1980.

[3]*The Spotlight,* July 23, 1981.

CHAPTER 11

[1]Robert S. Boyd, *The Charlotte Observer,* June 5, 1982, page 1.

[2]*U.S. News & World Report,* September 27, 1982, page 18.

CHAPTER 12

[1]Wright Patman, *A Primer on Money,* U.S. Government Printing Office, Washington, D.C., 1964, page 20.

[2]*Ibid.,* page 21.

[3]*The Spotlight,* 300 Independence Avenue, S.E., Washington, D.C. 20003.

CHAPTER 14

[1]*Break Free With 23 News,* P.O. Box 2386, El Cajon, California 92021, June 1982, page 8.

[2]*Mountain Lakes Shopper,* P.O. Box 1161, Andrews, North Carolina 28901, December 24, 1982, page 6.

[2]*Mountain Lakes Shopper,* P.O. Box 1161, Andrews, North Carolina 28901, December 24, 1982, page 6.

Index

A

Accord Agreement of 1951, 46
Aldrich, Nelson, 31-34
Aldrich-Vreeland Act of 1908, 31
Amalgamated Copper, 29
American Express, 105
Anderson, Jack, 97

B

Bank Holding Companies, 87-90
Bank of America, 97
Bank of New York, 13
barter, 3, 8
Baruch, Bernard, 34
Belmont, Auguste, 24
Bible, 3, 86, 123, 155
Bills of Exchange, 90-91
Black Friday 1869, 25, 92
Brazil, 107
Bretton Woods Conference, 1944, 94-96
Brooks, Pat, 125-126, 154
Bryan, William Jennings, 26
Burns, Arthur, 81-82

C

Canada, 108, 124-125
Charlotte Observer, 73-74, 85, 88
Chase (Secretary of Treasury), 21, 23
Chase Manhattan Bank, 83, 87-89, 97-100, 121
Chemical Bank of New York, 88
Christian Science Monitor, 86, 90
Citibank, 87
Citicorp, 67
Civil War, 19-23, 126-127
Clearing House Certificates, 30
Cleveland Panic, 26, 92
coins, 4, 8, 10, 14, 19, 24, 43, 91, 117-118
Coldwell Banker and Company, 105
Colonial Assembly, Congress, 10-12
Colonial Bills of Credit, 10-12
Commerical Bank Profits, 73-75
Congress, U.S., 14-19, 22, 24-27, 31, 33, 35, 42-44, 46, 64, 97, 126-140, 152, 171

R

Rarick, Congressman John, 69
Rate of Foreign Exchange, 90-91
Reader's Digest, 102
Reagan, Ronald, 107, 113, 153
representative government, 7
Republican Party, 33-34, 132
Resumption Act of 1749, 10
Return of the Puritans, The, 125-126, 154
Reuss, Henry, 83
Revolution, War of Independence, etc., 7, 12
Rockefeller Brothers of New York, 94, 96, 121
Rockefeller, David, 83, 96, 99
Romania, 102
Roosevelt, F.D., 46, 95
Roosevelt, Theodore, 30
Rothschild, Baron James, 24
Rothschilds, House of, 26, 88, 121
Russia, 100

S

Schiff, Jacob, 34
Sears Roebuck & Company, 105
Shearson, Loch Rhodes, 105
Shirley, Governor (1742), 9-10
silver, 4, 8, 10, 19, 92, 118
Silver Certificates, 25-26, 92
Singapore, 144
South America, 107
Special Drawing Rights, 93-94, 121
Spotlight, The, 87, 98, 102, 104-105, 144
Stockman, David, 102
Stock Market, 41-42, 100
Super Now Accounts, 104
Supreme Court, 131, 134
Swiss banks, 97

T

Taxes, 148, 151-153
Taylor, Col. Dick, 21

Thomas, Sen. Elmer, 42-43
Time Deposits, 71
Townsend, Jim, 64
Trilateral Commission, 98, 113
Truman, Harry, 46

U

Union Copper Company, 29
United States Bank, 15-17
United States Notes, 19-24, 46-48, 77, 126-127, 141
United States Treasury Banks, 138-143, 145-148
U.S. News & World Report, 100-102, 112
Untermyer, Samuel, 34

V

Vanderlip, Frank, 32, 34
Van Tyne, Claude, 7
Vietnam War, 91
Volcker, Paul A., 83, 106, 112

W

Warburg, Paul, 32-33
Watt, James, 101
White, Harry Dexter, 95
William III, 9
Wilson, Woodrow, 30-32, 34-35
World Bank, 102
World War I, 44
World War II, 46

Y

Yalta, 95